AN INSPECTOR DE SILVA MYSTERY

TROUBLE IN NUALA

HARRIET STEEL

Other Books by Harriet Steel

Becoming Lola

Salvation

City of Dreams

Following the Dream

Author's Note

Last year, I had the great good fortune to visit the island of Sri Lanka, the former Ceylon. I fell in love with the country straight away, awed by its tremendous natural beauty and the charm and friendliness of its people. I had been planning to write a new detective series for some time and when I came home, I decided to set it in Ceylon in the 1930s, a time when British Colonial rule created interesting contrasts, and sometimes conflicts, with traditional culture. Thus, Inspector Shanti de Silva and his friends were born.

As always, I am eternally grateful to my husband, Roger, for his encouragement and support. Heartfelt thanks are due to my daughter Ellie as well. Her professional advice has done so much to improve this novel. My thanks also go to Alan Jenkins for his expert advice on cricket. Any mistakes are my own.

If any characters resemble persons living or dead, this is purely coincidental. The town of Nuala is also fictitious.

Some readers have mentioned that an explanation of a few unfamiliar culinary terms would be helpful. I hope the following are of use:

A hopper: a kind of crispy pancake cooked in a bowl shape. It's usually served at breakfast with egg or curry in it.

String hoppers: noodles.

Brinjal: a special curry dish made from eggplant (aubergine).

Readers from countries where cricket is not played have also pointed out that some of the references in the novel are rather obscure to them. The lore and rules of cricket would fill volumes, and this is a murder mystery not a guide, but I hope a few pointers will help.

In amateur and one day matches, the convention is that the team who win the toss and choose whether to bat or bowl first declare their score (so many runs for the number of players caught or bowled out) roughly halfway through the day, allowing equal time for the other team to change over.

Googlies, leg spin and top spinners occur when a spin bowler uses various kinds of wrist action to deliver the ball in different ways in an attempt to confuse the batsman and bowl him out by hitting the wicket he is guarding.

Lbw – as well as being bowled out, or caught out by a fielder, the umpire may rule a batsman out lbw (leg before wicket) if he considers that the ball would have hit the wicket had it not hit some part of the batsman's body (usually the leg) first.

Note on language: the main three languages spoken on the island are Sinhalese, Tamil, and English. An educated man like Shanti de Silva would speak all three.

CHAPTER 1

Ceylon
February 1934

Inspector Shanti de Silva exhaled a deep sigh of relief as the train left the sweltering lowlands of Colombo and commenced the long climb to Kandy. From his seat in the polished teak and leather comfort of the railway carriage, he watched the forest become denser with every mile, plantations of banana, king coconut and rubber trees jostling for space in the rich, red earth.

From time to time, the trees retreated to make way for the startling lime-green splash of a paddy field where egrets stood like white question marks, hungry for water snails and frogs. Elsewhere he saw dusty villages slumbering in the heat of the afternoon. Their elders squatted outside the huts, huddled in little oases of shade cast by overhanging roofs thatched with palm leaves. Village children, their energy less sapped by the heat, jumped up and ran alongside the tracks waving and shouting until they tired of the race to keep up.

The train stopped at Kandy, obliging de Silva to pay for a rickshaw man to take him on to the nearby station at Peradeniya where he had to wait an hour for the hill train. Even in the waiting room, there was no escape from the heat. It seemed to have coalesced into a damp solid block that pressed down on the air, squeezing out every trace of freshness. He pushed a finger between the limp collar of his starched shirt and his perspiring neck and ran it around, then fanned himself with his hat.

A summons to attend as a witness in a trial at the High Court in Colombo had been the cause of this uncongenial journey. He consoled himself with the thought that his evidence had made a considerable contribution to the conviction of a gang of thieves who would no longer be at liberty to ply their nefarious trade in the city's bazaars and public places. It had been a nuisance though that the trial had run into an extra day. He had hoped to be home for the weekend, but it hadn't been practical to make the slow journey after Friday's hearing only to return on Sunday in time for court the following day.

He looked at the clock on the waiting room wall. How was it possible that only ten minutes had passed? A chai wallah passed the door and de Silva called him in and handed over a few annas in exchange for a battered tin cup of tea. The brew was more stewed than he liked, but it gave some relief to his parched throat.

He thought wistfully of the cool drawing room at Sunnybank, the pleasant bungalow built in the English style where his wife would be waiting. Jane always served tea in the bone china cups they had been given for a wedding present. Cook would be instructed to make finger sandwiches filled with finely sliced cucumber and hard-boiled egg; slices of his favourite butter cake would tempt his appetite. He drained the brackish tea and closed his eyes. Leaning back against the bench, he fell into a doze.

Thirty minutes later, the tinny sound of the clock striking the hour woke him. A moment passed before he remembered where he was and jumped up briskly. Out on the platform a gaggle of other travellers waited, a few of them Europeans who appeared to be suffering from the heat even more than he was; the rest were locals. The men wore loose, white cotton trousers and tunics and the women colourful saris. They seemed in festive spirits. Hindus, he guessed, going up to the Sita temple.

The hill train came into sight and a short time passed while it unloaded its passengers and edged its way onto the turntable to be turned around ready to begin its last climb of the day. Despite the number of times he had made the journey, de Silva felt a pleasant rush of anticipation as he took his seat. The trains on the line up to Nanu Oya where he would alight for his home at Nuala were not as modern and comfortable as those on the Colombo–Kandy line, but the views were magnificent.

In fact, he reflected, the whole line was a miracle of engineering. Something the British must be given credit for. Relentless gradients, walls of rock, and steep hillsides had not stood in the way of those doughty Victorians who had come from their damp, misty isle to colonise his own lush exotic one. When the coffee they had first planted in the hill country failed, they had turned their energies to cultivating tea. Now Ceylon supplied half the world.

The train lumbered higher and higher, and the tea terraces came into view. Endless vistas of vivid green made up of gracefully curving, neat lines of bushes, kept low so that the supply of leaves that the women pluckers took would always be newly sprouted and tender. Here and there were small lakes, their surfaces smothered with water lilies.

By the time they reached Nanu Oya, the beauty of it all had fully restored de Silva's good humour. He stepped out from the station and smiled at the sight that met his eyes. The last rays of the sun gleamed on the dark-blue paintwork and spotless chrome of the Morris Cowley 2-Seater Tourer, his most beloved possession, except of course, his darling wife.

Jayasena, the only servant he trusted to drive the Morris,

held the driver's door open for him to get in. De Silva gestured to his bags and as he slid into the seat, inhaling the aromas of leather and wax polish, Jayasena strapped them on the back. Moments later the engine roared into life. The gearstick moved into first like a hot knife into butter and the Morris glided forward. He liked to boast that she could reach a top speed of forty-five miles per hour, but that opportunity only arose when the roads of Nuala were empty of rickshaws and buffalo carts for one of the town's celebrated rallies. This afternoon they proceeded at a stately twenty in the direction of Sunnybank.

* * *

'Jane? I'm home!'

He strode into the drawing room where his wife looked up from her book with a smile and offered him her cheek to kiss. 'So you are. How was Colombo?'

'Hot. Noisy. The air full of dust as usual.'

She made a face, reached for the small brass bell on the table at her side and rang it briskly. 'I'll ask for tea to be got ready.'

'Excellent. I'll go and wash in the meantime.'

A servant appeared in the doorway and Jane de Silva nodded to her. 'Please tell cook to serve tea in fifteen minutes, Sria.'

'Yes, memsahib.'

Half an hour later, fortified by tea and scones with thick cream and wood apple jam, de Silva recounted the events in Colombo's High Court that had led to ten members of the Black Lotus gang being put behind bars for the next twenty years.

'The first case you were working on when I met you,' his wife mused when he reached the end. 'I must admit, I was afraid for you sometimes. Some of these Hong Kong Chinese are such violent people.'

'Certainly, the criminal element is. And that is precisely why we don't want them here.' De Silva helped himself to another scone and slathered it with jam and cream. He took a bite and patted his stomach. 'These are too good. I shall have to ration myself in future.'

His wife raised an eyebrow. 'You've said that before, dear.'

He chuckled. 'I'll take a turn around the garden before dinner. That will make all the difference.'

In a far corner of the garden, Anif the gardener was engaged in the perpetual task of sweeping up, his broom making a faint scratching noise through the dry leaves. De Silva felt the springiness of the lawn under his feet. He smelled the sweet aromas of frangipani and jasmine and all the many scents of his roses: musk, apricot, spice, honey, even tea. He had always had a good sense of smell and he picked each one out with ease. What a lucky man he was to have all this to enjoy.

His prized roses stood in glossy profusion in their beds, immaculately tended by Anif under his instruction to produce only the finest flowers. Beyond the clipped privet hedge, a tidy vegetable garden contained straight rows of carrots, beans, peas, potatoes, and eggplants. If only such ordered and productive beauty characterised all human affairs.

He touched a deep-red, velvety bloom. The rose *Black Prince* was one of his favourites, and not just on account of its colour and scent. For him, the name conjured up romantic visions of medieval castles where armoured knights jousted and ladies in embroidered gowns waited in ivory towers. An England of Gothic cathedrals where sumptuously robed clergy processed down candlelit naves to the strains of solemn music. It was the England he liked to imagine, even if Jane laughed and told him that the reality was far more complicated.

'There are lovely places, but a lot of England is ugly. We have plenty of poor housing and dingy streets, as well as factories with chimneys belching smoke.'

'Just like Colombo then.'

'But not so hot.'

De Silva ran his fingertips over the cool, moist petals of another rose, this one the palest of shell pinks. Well, whatever England was really like, he would never cease to thank the gods that Jane had left it and come to Colombo as governess to one of the British families. He had been part of the Colombo force then. The moment he had set eyes on her, he'd known she was the one for him. Both in their forties, with no relations to tut over the unsuitability of a marriage between a Sinhalese Buddhist, who might also owe some of his bloodline to a Portuguese settler from the dim and distant past, and an Anglican Englishwoman, they had been free to please themselves. The offer of promotion and a job in the cooler climate of Nuala had been the perfect wedding gift.

He snapped off one of the *Black Prince's* flowers and added a few from other bushes to make a posy for Jane, then with a last look around the garden already dissolving in the purple twilight, he started back for the bungalow.

CHAPTER 2

'Are you going to work today, dear?' asked Jane the following morning.

A gently baked egg smiled up at de Silva from the bottom of his crispy bowl-shaped breakfast hopper. He broke off a piece of the pancake, dipped it into the egg yolk and nodded. 'I have to write up my report, but I hope there won't be any need to stay long. If anything important happened while I was away, no doubt Prasanna would have sent a message.'

He reached for the china dish beside his cup and saucer and ladled a spoonful of fiery sambal relish onto his egg. Jane raised her eyebrows. Even after five years in Ceylon, two of them as his wife, she still wasn't comfortable with the idea of eating chillies at breakfast.

'But sambal is delicious with egg, and the hotter the better.'

'So you keep telling me.'

'Never mind. If you prefer your milk rolls and jam, then that is what you must have.' He polished off the last of the hopper, wiped his mouth and pushed back his chair. 'I'll be back as quickly as I can. I thought we might have a picnic by the lake. If you have no other plans for the afternoon, that is.'

'Lovely. I only need to return a book to the library. I hear they've just got in a copy of the new Agatha Christie. I want to borrow it before Florence Clutterbuck does.'

He chuckled.

'Have I said something amusing?'

He came around to her side of the table and kissed her cheek. 'Enjoy your morning. And please resist the temptation to murder the assistant government agent's wife if she reaches the library before you.'

'What nonsense you talk, dear.'

'I do my best.'

* * *

The Morris soon left behind the quiet road on the edge of town where Sunnybank was situated, and de Silva was obliged to slow to negotiate the morning chaos of Nuala's traffic. Rickshaws darted between bullock carts laden with sacks of rice, piles of bananas and coconuts, and mounds of other fruits and vegetables. Stalls offering cooked food lined the dusty streets and passers-by stopped to purchase bowls of curry and rice or paper cornets of sticky sweetmeats.

The front of a shop that dispensed Ayurvedic remedies was bright with garlands of marigolds and gaudy pictures of smiling customers. Crammed in the display case under the counter, a multitude of bottles and jars contained medicinal herbs and spices. A few doors along the street, he glimpsed bales of jewel-coloured silk in the dark interior of a sari shop. At roadside shrines, statues of the Buddha sat in serene meditation amid jumbles of incense burners, candles, and offerings of lotus flowers. In the distance the surface of the town lake gleamed like a sheet of silver.

It was the British contribution to Nuala's amenities that marked it as different from a typical Ceylonese town. The assistant government agent's residence was a large and elegant white house with a classical portico. It was set off by English-style gardens with immaculate lawns. The golf club would have been equally at home under English skies. The post office boasted a clock tower that looked like the spire of an English country church and finally there was the Crown Hotel, a sprawling, mock-Tudor edifice that dominated one corner of the crossroads where it was situated.

The door to the police station was unlocked but no one was about. De Silva glanced around the public room. Evidence of recent tea-making indicated that Sergeant Prasanna and Constable Nadar were not far away.

He called out and receiving no answer went into his office. It too was empty. Frowning, he returned to the public room and followed the passage leading to the yard at the back of the station. As sunlight and heat met him, he heard the sound of leather on willow and a shout of "Howzat!"

Constable Nadar squinted at his colleague. 'I wasn't ready,' he protested. Sergeant Prasanna, the brightest star of the Nuala cricket team, grinned. 'Then put the stumps back up and I'll bowl you out again.'

He polished the ball on his khaki shorts then noticed de Silva. His face fell. 'Inspector de Silva... we weren't expecting...'

'So I see.'

'We haven't been out here long, sir. Just a bit of a break. It's the match against Hatton on Saturday.'

'Well, you had better win it.'

'Yes, sir.'

The sergeant grinned sheepishly, and de Silva suppressed a smile. 'Back to work, both of you. Prasanna, have you found the owners of those stray ponies that are making a nuisance of themselves down by the lake yet?'

'No, sir.'

'Then get on with it. And if you have nothing better to do, you can master the finer points of the Departmental Order Book and explain them to me.'

'Yes, sir.'

'Oh and bring some tea to my office.'

'Right-ho, sir.'

De Silva shook his head. '*Yes*, sir, Sergeant.'

'Sorry, sir.'

In his office he sipped his tea and leafed through the pile of papers on his desk. There was nothing that needed dealing with immediately. He turned his attention to writing the report of his part in the Black Lotus trial. When it was complete, he leant back in his chair with his hands behind his head and stretched. If he left in the next half an hour, he would be at home in plenty of time for a trip to the lake.

He read through the report once more, stood up and took it over to one of the metal filing cabinets that lined a wall of the room. He pulled out a drawer and walked two fingers through the dividers until he reached the letter "B" then, the report safe in its proper place, he dusted off his hands and closed the drawer. He wondered briefly if it would ever see the light of day again. Probably not, nevertheless protocols had to be observed and tiresome as they sometimes were, they satisfied his sense of order.

His thoughts dwelt on the Black Lotus gang as he straightened his desk and refilled his pens for the morning. Rising from the slums and go-downs of Hong Kong, the secret society that the Chinese called a triad was said to have a hand in a vast number of Asia's gambling and smuggling rackets. Many of the bodies washed up in harbours from Hong Kong to Bombay were reputed to be their handiwork. The flushing out of the chapter who had sought to practise their dark arts in Ceylon had been a major triumph for Colombo's police force. He was proud to have played his part. But he was also extremely glad that those days were over. A quiet life in Nuala suited him very well.

He shrugged on the uniform jacket he had removed

while he was writing and patted the elephant badge on the lapel. When he was a boy, elephants had been plentiful in Ceylon. He grimaced. That was something the country didn't thank the British for. All their needless hunting – killing out of arrogance and conceit. It was an aspect of the British character he disliked intensely. What profit did they gain from massacring a hundred, two hundred or even a thousand elephants? The lives of those magnificent creatures were nothing to them but the raw material for boasting of their exploits at their clubs.

He took a breath and his shoulders dropped. Of course, not all the British were like that. Many were like his Jane, fond of the country and appreciating all the beauty and variety with which nature had blessed it. Change would come one day, and it was right that it should, but it might be a mistake to push the British out too soon, as the activists wanted. Change was best when it came gradually, not like a tropical storm smashing down all but the sturdiest trees in its path.

His hand was on the doorknob when the black Bakelite telephone on his desk erupted into life. With a sigh, he picked up the receiver, hoping the call wouldn't sound the death knell of his plans for the afternoon. The gruff voice of his boss, the assistant government agent, crackled down the line. 'De Silva?'

'Mr Clutterbuck, sir. What can I do for you?'

De Silva listened for a few moments, the crease between his brows deepening. 'I see… yes… of course… in half an hour.'

He made a quick telephone call home, leaving a message for Jane who was still out, and set off.

CHAPTER 3

The Morris turned off the public road into the driveway leading up to the Residence. As he slowed to round the bends, de Silva wondered what it was that made Clutterbuck want to see him at such short notice. He parked the car in the shade and went up to the Residence's imposing front door. One of the house servants answered the bell.

'The master is on the telephone,' the man said. 'He asks if you will wait in the hall.'

De Silva nodded and sat down in one of the easy chairs. He looked about him and thought what a lovely place the assistant government agent's home was. The British did themselves proud in Ceylon. The floor was of well-aged teak, polished to a deep lustre, the furniture was antique and the hangings and carvings on the wall were of fine quality. Someone had arranged a bowl of jasmine on a side table and its perfume filled the air.

The quiet was broken by the creak of footsteps and the click of toenails on wood. Archie Clutterbuck came through the doorway, followed by his elderly black Labrador, Darcy.

'Ah! Inspector de Silva. Good of you to come so promptly. Forgive me for hijacking your afternoon.'

The assistant government agent's jowly face and heavy-set build often gave people the impression that he would be intimidating but de Silva had usually found him fair and reasonable to deal with. He jumped to his feet. 'There's no need to apologise, sir. There was nothing that couldn't be postponed.'

Darcy sniffed his hand, and de Silva felt a wet nose.

'Don't make a nuisance of yourself, old chap,' Clutterbuck scolded. 'Push him off if you like, de Silva. He always thinks everyone wants to be his friend, although it's not necessarily the case.'

'It's not a problem, sir. I like dogs, even though we don't have one ourselves.'

'Good. Well, shall we go to my study? We can talk in peace there.'

Slightly mystified, de Silva followed Clutterbuck along a passage lined with hunting prints. The study was a very masculine room, the furniture battered in comparison with the elegant pieces in the hall. It was also very untidy with piles of papers and periodicals stacked on every surface. Many of the latter were magazines for the sportsman and fisherman. Clutterbuck's fondness for trout fishing in the clear waters of the rivers up at Horton Plains was well known. A strong smell of tobacco permeated the air.

The Labrador went over to the fireplace and flopped down on the Indian rug in front of the hearth. He rested his chin on his paws, but his eyes remained open, following his master's every move. Clutterbuck leant down to pat him, and his tail thumped.

'Will you have a whisky, Inspector? I usually have a pre-prandial.'

This was a British habit that de Silva had not found it hard to adopt, even coming to prefer the drink to arrack. 'Thank you, sir. I will.'

'Take a seat. Make yourself comfortable.'

De Silva sat down in an armchair whose springs had known better days as Clutterbuck poured generous measures into two cut-glass tumblers and handed him one of them. He indicated a small ebony box inlaid with ivory. 'Cigarette?'

'Thank you, no.'

'Mind if I do?'

'Not at all.'

De Silva suppressed a twinge of impatience. Unless this was a purely social visit, and he doubted that, he wished Clutterbuck would get to the point.

The assistant government agent lit up a Passing Cloud and inhaled as he shook out the match.

'Well, to business. I expect you're wondering why I asked you here.' He cleared his throat and de Silva waited. 'It's a rather tricky matter,' he went on at last. 'One of the planters may have gone a bit too far with one of his people.' He drained his glass. 'Another?'

De Silva shook his head.

'The thing is, the government agent was back off to Kandy the day it came up, but before he left, he told me he wanted the whole wretched business sorted out sharpish in case the situation got ugly.'

De Silva pictured William Petrie barking the order before the official car whisked him off to the provincial capital at Kandy.

'Who is the man involved?'

'Renshaw. Charles Renshaw.'

De Silva recognised the name. Charles Renshaw had come to the area about a year previously when he inherited his plantation from a distant relative. Few people had a good word to say for him.

In general, de Silva had to admit that Renshaw was the exception to the rule. Most of the tea plantation owners treated their workers reasonably well nowadays. They worked long hours, but they were given breaks and adequate food. Healthcare was provided, albeit of a fairly basic nature, and if a worker was genuinely sick and unable to go out to the fields, he or she was not penalised for it. There was still room for improvement, but changing things too quickly tended to invite trouble. Renshaw was, however, reputed to be a boss who wasn't taking any steps towards a better future.

'What happened?'

'Allegedly, Renshaw flogged one of his workers, a man called Hari Gooptu. Renshaw denied it and said Gooptu was malingering, claiming he'd trodden on a stray nail on the factory floor that had flown off one of the machines and he was unable to walk.'

De Silva winced at the thought. 'And was he?'

'According to Renshaw there wasn't much wrong with him, and he'd driven the nail into his foot deliberately to avoid working. Apparently, he's been a troublemaker for some time.'

'But flogging…'

'Quite; but whatever the truth about Gooptu, and at the moment we have no proof he was flogged, the Tamils are used to a firm hand. It doesn't do to upset that. If there was to be a strike it could spread and then where would we be?'

'Is there any indication there will be?'

'Not yet, but what concerns me is the confidential information I've received about the Colombo lawyer interesting himself in the business. He's a local chap and reputed to be very clever – probably too clever for his own good. They tell me in Colombo that they've had their eye on him for a while. A higher education doesn't necessarily fit a man to understand every situation. Questioning the actions of one of the planters is likely to open up a most undesirable can of worms. Best to rely on them to do the right thing. Most of 'em do.'

'Do you think this man will stir up Renshaw's workers?'

'It's not beyond the bounds of possibility.'

De Silva frowned. Inevitably, Clutterbuck would look at things from the British point of view and not want to make trouble for Renshaw, but if Gooptu had been ill-treated, it was wrong to let the planter get away with it.

Clutterbuck had the grace to colour a little. 'One rogue doesn't change things in my view, and I'm satisfied that will be the government agent's view too. A stiff warning ought to be sufficient to bring Renshaw into line.'

He went to the sideboard and picked up the whisky bottle. 'A drop more?'

'Thank you, but I won't.'

'I think I'll have a small one.'

'And the lawyer's name is?'

'Tagore. Ravindra Tagore.'

It was an unusual name for this part of the world. 'What has brought him up to Nuala?'

'I'm not certain. Some family business, I believe. It's most unfortunate it's coincided with this. Anyway as I say, William Petrie wants it knocked on the head as soon as possible. I'd like you to go and see Renshaw first.'

'Might it not be better for you to have a quiet word?'

'I think it's rather late for that. I hear Tagore is already preparing a formal request for an investigation. I thought you might already have received it but clearly not. If we're seen to be trying to apply political pressure, it could only make matters worse.'

'I understand.'

'Good man. Report to me on what you find and then we can decide how to handle Tagore.'

Clutterbuck drained his glass and stood up. Darcy scrambled to his feet, tail wagging. 'Thank you for your time, de Silva. I hope to hear from you soon.'

'You will, sir.'

As he left the Residence to return to the Morris, de Silva felt a pang of irritation. Clutterbuck was by no means the worst of the British he had come across in his career. Some of them rode roughshod over the local officials whereas he had the decency to give the impression of consulting rather than commanding. However, the fact remained that in practice the assistant government agent would have the last word.

CHAPTER 4

Jane sat in the garden in the shade of the frangipani tree. He dropped a kiss on her cheek. 'I'm sorry about the picnic.'

'Never mind. What did Archie Clutterbuck want?'

De Silva glanced at the cover of the Agatha Christie detective novel in his wife's lap. 'He demanded to know why his wife had a black eye.'

'You and your nonsense. What did he really want?'

'There's some trouble at one of the plantations – Charles Renshaw's place.'

She frowned. 'That awful man? His wife comes to church. She's a pretty little thing but looks as if she'd be afraid of her own shadow. I ought to make more effort to talk to her, poor girl. She might be glad of a friend. I wouldn't be surprised if her husband bullies her.'

'You may be right but that's not what Clutterbuck wanted to talk about.'

'It's shameful that innocent people are treated so badly,' she said when de Silva had explained.

'We don't know yet whether this man was telling the truth.'

'If he was, I hope you'll throw the book at Renshaw. Flogging is barbaric. We're living in the 1930s, not the Middle Ages.'

'I agree with you. Please don't be in any doubt about that. If the man was flogged, it will be made clear to Renshaw that it's not to happen again, not unless he wants me on his tail. He'll have to find other means of keeping his workers in line.'

'Paying them better and improving their living quarters perhaps,' his wife said acerbically.

'We live in an imperfect world, my love. At least the Tamil workers on the plantations have a wage and a roof over their heads. On the whole they're better off than they would be if they'd stayed in India.'

'Shanti! Aren't you making rather light of this?'

'As I said, we don't even know if the allegation's true yet. And I have to bear it in mind that my job is also to keep the peace. Clutterbuck's concerned that if Renshaw was to be charged and word got around the plantations, it might stir up trouble with the workers. He believes that if there's anything in this accusation, a warning shot across the ship would be a better way of dealing with it and enough to make Renshaw think twice about his actions.'

'Across the bows, dear.' Jane sighed. 'I suppose Archie Clutterbuck may have a point. We don't know the true circumstances and a warning might be the best way to start.'

She closed her book, set it down on the table beside her and stood up. 'I'd better go and talk to cook about dinner.' She paused for a moment then, 'You know, I think I recall this man Tagore from my days in Colombo. Do you remember that the father of the family I worked for was a professor of law?'

'Yes.'

'Well, quite a few of his students used to be invited to the house if there was a party or a dinner. I'm sure Tagore was one of them. He was studying to be a barrister. Such a handsome young man. He had lovely dark-brown eyes and curly hair that was black as ink. He spoke English perfectly.'

'It sounds like I was lucky to snatch you from him.'

She laughed. 'Oh, he was never more than an acquaintance and he would have been far too young for me anyway.

And a little too serious.' She caught his eye. 'I do believe you're jealous.'

He put his arm around her waist and gave it a squeeze. 'I'm jealous of any man who might turn your head, my dear.'

She leant her cheek on his shoulder. 'You know perfectly well that no one could.'

'I'm glad to hear it. Now, I don't know about dinner, but I've had no lunch.'

'Then I'll tell cook to send you out something to keep you going.'

They chatted as he ate the snacks that Sria brought out. Later as the shadows on the lawn lengthened and a breeze stirred, rustling the leaves of the coconut palms, they went inside. The evenings were still chilly in February. As usual, after dinner the fire in the drawing room was lit. The warmth made him sleepy and the book he read failed to hold his attention. He had to admit, it wasn't the author's fault. The prospect of dealing with Charles Renshaw kept coming between him and Sir Walter Scott's stirring tale.

Jane turned the last page of her Agatha Christie and closed the book. 'As good as ever,' she remarked. 'But you don't seem much struck with *Ivanhoe*.'

He shrugged. 'I'm a bit too preoccupied, I suppose.'

'Poor dear. A good night's sleep often unravels problems. Shall we get to bed?'

'Good idea.'

She rested her chin on one hand. 'If you meet Mr Tagore, it will be interesting to see how he's turned out. I wonder if he married. There were certainly plenty of girls in Colombo who seemed willing.'

'If I meet him, I promise to carry out a detailed forensic examination of his personal life for you, my love.'

She picked up the cushion at her elbow and tossed it at him. 'Don't you dare!'

CHAPTER 5

De Silva drove to the station the following morning under a sapphire sky. Constable Nadar was bent diligently over his work when he arrived. He jumped to his feet. 'Good morning, sir.'

'Anything to report?'

'A man came in earlier wanting to see you, sir. I told him we weren't expecting you for another hour and he said he'd come back.'

'Did he say what he wanted?'

'No, sir.'

'What sort of person was he?'

'Quite a young man, sir, tall and well dressed.'

'Did he give his name?'

'He said it was Tagore.'

'Ah. You'd better send him in to me when he comes back. Where's Sergeant Prasanna?'

'He went down to the lake to see about the ponies, sir.'

'Good. I'll have my tea now.' He glanced at the papers in front of Nadar. 'What's that one about?'

'From one of the Ayurvedic doctors, sir. He has a stall on one of the side streets. The lock of his premises was broken when he came to open up yesterday. Nothing seems to have been taken that he could see, but bottles and jars on the shelves had been moved around and someone had been through the drawers underneath and emptied a few packets of spices and herbs on the ground.'

'Odd. It doesn't sound like it's worth wasting much time on but tell the man we'll make inquiries. Probably just teenagers larking about.'

'It's quite likely, sir. Between ourselves, he's not a popular man in his neighbourhood.'

In his office de Silva drank his tea and mulled over how he would deal with his visitor. The lawyer didn't waste much time. He looked at the clock and decided that he might as well get this meeting over with and dispense with the idea of visiting Renshaw first. The difficulty was that he sympathised with the lawyer's view on flogging. It was unacceptable, but Tagore was likely to overestimate what he, de Silva, could do about it. These planters were gods on their own plantations. Pressure from their superiors or peers, self-interest or, in the best examples, goodwill might lead them to treat their workers decently, but it was very unlikely that a judge would find against them unless a worker was seriously injured or killed. Renshaw was not such a fool as to risk that. A whole system that had been more than a hundred years in the making couldn't be swept away overnight, although sometimes he wished it could.

There was a knock at the door and Constable Nadar put his head around it. 'Mr Tagore to see you, sir, if it's convenient.'

'Send him in, Constable.'

De Silva rose to his feet. With an unconscious movement, he straightened the elephant badge on his lapel.

Ravindra Tagore made a striking figure with his handsome features and tall frame. Jane had said he was a law student when she met him in Colombo, so he must be in his late twenties now. It looked as if the intervening years had not been easy ones. His eyes had a world-weary expression, and faint lines were etched on his forehead. De Silva decided to say nothing of his meeting with the assistant government agent for the moment.

'Mr Tagore! Please take a seat. What can I do for you?'

Tagore sat down. He exuded an air of natural authority that de Silva found irksome. It brought to mind the run-ins he recalled having with members of the Colombo Bar in the old days. Some lawyers had a way of thinking they were a cut above the police, and of overestimating their clients' innocence.

'I wish to make a complaint against Mr Charles Renshaw. You know him, I presume.'

'I know of him. He has a tea plantation not far from here.'

Tagore nodded.

'And what is the nature of your complaint, Mr Tagore? Has Charles Renshaw caused you loss in some way?'

'No, my complaint concerns his treatment of one of his workers.'

Ah, here it comes, thought de Silva.

'Renshaw accused the man of injuring himself deliberately and flogged him. Even if the injury was self-inflicted, and there is no evidence that it was, such a punishment is disproportionate and inhuman.'

De Silva rested his elbows on his desk and made a steeple with his fingers and thumbs. 'Mr Tagore, if I am to take this further, I need this man to come to me and tell his story.'

Tagore let out a snort of exasperation. 'I'm a lawyer, Inspector de Silva. I'm fully aware of the legal process involved.'

'Does the man intend to come here then?'

'He's an uneducated plantation worker, Inspector. Such people are usually afraid of their employers, but let me put it to you – does that mean they should be denied the same access to justice as other men? If I can talk to this man, I'm sure I can persuade him to speak up for himself.'

'So why haven't you done so?'

'Because Renshaw refuses to give me access to him which is in itself suspicious. Something he won't be at liberty to do if you investigate the case.'

'Did he tell you why?'

'He told me the man had gone back to his village, but I wasn't convinced that was the truth.' He hesitated. 'In fact it has crossed my mind there's a far more sinister reason why Renshaw won't allow me to interview him.'

De Silva frowned. This complaint was becoming more serious than Clutterbuck had led him to believe.

'Do you mean murder? Come, come, Mr Tagore. A lawyer of all people should be more circumspect about rushing to conclusions that might lay him open to a charge of slander.'

'I hope I can trust that you'll treat anything said in this room as being in confidence,' said Tagore stiffly.

De Silva leant back in his chair and tapped his cheek with one finger. After a moment or two of withstanding Tagore's expression of withering scorn, he pulled a pad of paper towards him, picked up a pen and made a note. It was a trick he often used to buy time to compose himself.

He stopped writing and regarded Tagore calmly. 'Your concern is laudable, Mr Tagore. I can't promise anything, but I will pay a call on Renshaw and find out more about what happened. But if this man—'

'Gooptu – Hari Gooptu.'

'If this man Gooptu has nothing to say for himself, it must be the end of the matter.'

'And what if you don't find him?'

'Mr Tagore—'

Tagore was already reaching into the bag he had brought with him. He pulled out what looked like a grimy bundle of cloth and held it up for de Silva's inspection. It was a coarsely woven shirt of the kind plantation workers wore, but more significantly, it was heavily stained with blood.

'I think it can be said with justification that this provides persuasive evidence that in any event Renshaw has a case to answer.'

'Who does it belong to?'

'Hari Gooptu.'

'You're sure about that? Did he give it to you himself? How can that be if you've not met him?'

For a moment Tagore looked uncomfortable.

'It came from another source.'

'Another source? You'll need to be more specific than that. Who was it?'

'I'm not at liberty to say.'

Briefly, de Silva deliberated. From the set of Tagore's expression, he was obviously going to persist, and if the shirt did belong to Gooptu, there was a strong possibility it was at least evidence that he had been flogged.

'Very well, Mr Tagore,' he said at last. 'As I say, I'll speak to Renshaw. If I think it appropriate, I'll give him a warning.'

'And that will be all?'

The hairs on the back of de Silva's neck prickled. 'It's all I'm prepared to say at the moment.'

'When he should at least be charged with causing grievous bodily harm.'

'You've not yet proved what he did, Mr Tagore. I'll need hard evidence to confirm your accusations. But I will speak to Renshaw. If there's any truth in the matter, I hope a warning will suffice.'

He scribbled another note on the pad of paper then looked up. 'Does that satisfy you?'

'No, but it doesn't surprise me. Don't rock the boat. It's a well-worn refrain.' Tagore unfolded his long legs and got to his feet. 'I see you're not prepared to take this seriously. Don't think you've heard the last of it.'

De Silva seethed. This man did him an injustice if he

believed he didn't care. Tagore was probably dramatizing the situation when he hinted at murder, but the idea of harsh punishment revolted de Silva as much as it did any decent man. If Gooptu had been flogged, he intended to make it clear to Renshaw that any more beatings would make charges likely to follow.

But de Silva's anger was tainted with guilt and a pain crept in behind his eyes. Why did the lawyer's zeal rile him? Was it because he feared that he had fallen in too readily with Clutterbuck's aim of dealing with the matter with as little fuss as possible?

He pushed the thought away. At this stage, the professional course was to keep a distance between himself and Tagore. There might be no truth in the matter, and as a policeman, he must deal in facts and the law. The extent to which a master could legally discipline his workers was one of degree. It would be hard to get a conviction without strong evidence that Renshaw had gone too far. If this man Gooptu was found but refused to come forward, it would be impossible. A bloodstained shirt from an anonymous source wouldn't change that.

And what if he wasn't found? De Silva groaned inwardly. Clutterbuck might have saddled him with an intractable problem. Tagore seemed a persistent fellow.

He turned his attention back to Tagore's grim face. 'I hope you aren't trying to threaten me, Mr Tagore.'

'I wouldn't dream of it, Inspector.'

The silence crackled. Eventually, de Silva decided to allow Tagore a small victory and be the first to break it.

'Are you staying long in Nuala?' he asked in a neutral tone that he hoped might defuse the tension a little. 'I may need to speak to you again.' Privately he thought that it would also be good to know for how much longer he would need to watch out for trouble from Mr Tagore.

'A week or so. My work in Colombo won't allow me to

be absent for long, but my mother died, and I have to settle her affairs.'

'Allow me to offer my condolences.'

Tagore's expression softened a fraction. 'Thank you. My parents lived here for many years. I had forgotten how beautiful the hill country is.'

'Were they born in Ceylon?' asked de Silva, snatching at an opportunity to take the sourness out of the conversation a little more.

'You're thinking of my name? More suitable to Bengal of course, but my family has always lived here in Ceylon. My father was a fervent admirer of the great poet and changed the original family name to Tagore in homage.'

'How interesting.'

Tagore hesitated, then as if he regretted disclosing a personal detail, he stood up and nodded curtly. 'Thank you for your time, Inspector. If you wish to speak to me, you'll find me at the Nuala Hotel.'

The door closed behind him, and de Silva sighed. Once he had been hot-headed and idealistic like Tagore, but as he'd grown older, the complexity of human affairs had taught him caution. Sometimes, however, he found it hard to decide whether that was really a good thing.

CHAPTER 6

The following morning it took him forty minutes to drive the ten miles to the Five Palms plantation. The monsoon looked to have washed away the last stretch of the narrow road and it must have been poorly repaired since already potholes and ruts made it treacherous. De Silva wondered whether it was inexperience or parsimony that had made Renshaw skimp on the work.

He passed the entrance to the plantation bungalow. Through the stone pillars on either side of the open gates he saw a sweep of unkempt lawn with the clump of lofty palms that presumably gave the place its name to one side. On the opposite side of the lawn squatted the bungalow. It needed a fresh coat of paint, and creepers rampaged over the walls and the roof. The remainder of the way up to the tea factory looked even more uninviting than the first part of the road so he eased the Morris onto the dusty verge, pulled up the hood and set off to walk.

He had to admit that whatever the plantation's short-comings, the view was magnificent. A panorama of vibrant green terraces rolled down the hillside. Women pluckers moved through the bushes like bright little sailing boats in an emerald sea. As he neared the factory, he saw some of them coming back from the fields carrying baskets of leaves on their backs.

The hum of machinery grew louder. In the covered area

outside the factory doors, some of the pluckers had already tipped their baskets out onto big canvas sheets and were sorting the tips from the coarser leaves with quick, nimble fingers that continued to flash through the green piles even as their owners cast him wary glances. A woman dressed in a better sari than the rest emerged from a nearby door.

'Is your master here?' de Silva asked.

She pointed to the factory building. He noticed that its condition was as shabby as the plantation bungalow's although as it was an industrial building there was perhaps more excuse.

The hum turned to a roar as de Silva entered. He nearly collided with a wiry man carrying two enormous sacks on his back. 'Where's the master?' de Silva shouted.

'The rolling room.' The man jerked his head in the direction of a door on the right then bounded away up a flight of metal stairs.

In the rolling room the noise of heavy machinery was overpowering. Fine, tea-scented dust filled the air. A few moments passed before de Silva's eyes adjusted to the dimmer light and he saw a stocky florid-faced man he guessed to be Renshaw. The man looked up from the handful of dry leaves he was examining, tossed them into the sack at his feet and came over to where de Silva stood.

'No strangers allowed in here,' he growled.

De Silva indicated his police badge. 'My name is Inspector de Silva. I'd be obliged if you'd spare me a moment of your time, sir.'

Renshaw nodded curtly. 'You'd better come to my office.'

The office was a bleak room with narrow metal windows; a sickly light filtered through their grimy panes. Furniture was scant and where the walls were not lined with filing cabinets and shelves crammed with papers, the paintwork was peeling. Cracked linoleum covered the floor.

Renshaw flopped down in the chair behind his desk but

didn't offer de Silva a seat. 'I haven't much time,' he said. 'We have a shipment due to go down to the tea auctions at Colombo tomorrow. Whatever this is about, you'd better make it brief.'

De Silva took a breath to suppress his irritation. Clearly, Renshaw was not going to be an easy man to deal with. At first glance it seemed eminently plausible that he would mistreat his workers.

'We've received information about one of your workers – a man named Hari Gooptu.'

Renshaw put up his hand with the palm towards de Silva. 'Stop there, Inspector. The man was nothing but a troublemaker. I suppose you were told he was wrongfully injured on the factory floor. That's a pack of lies. He engineered his "accident" to get out of working.'

He scratched his cheek. The smattering of a rash was visible on his sunburnt skin. In one place there was a weeping sore.

'And this isn't the first time,' he continued. 'I warned him he'd be out of a job if he tried anything on again, so I sent him packing. You have to keep to your word or forfeit these people's respect. Doubtless he's idling in some jungle village by now – I've no idea where – and good riddance.'

De Silva cursed inwardly. This was the worst possible scenario. Renshaw must have seen trouble coming and this was his way of sidestepping it, but was he telling the truth? De Silva thought of the bloodstained shirt Tagore had left with him. Useless to raise it at this stage. Renshaw was obviously far too wily not to question its authenticity as he had himself.

Renshaw's lips twitched in a half-smile. He stood up. 'Is that all, Inspector?'

'Not quite. Apparently, the man was flogged. I believe you're still quite new to this business, Mr Renshaw, but these days that level of discipline is considered unacceptable.'

A sour look came over Renshaw's face. 'I know what this is all about. It's that fellow Tagore, isn't it? I suppose he put you up to this. He was up here trying to interfere in my business a few days ago, making a lot of unfounded allegations about how Gooptu was treated.'

He scowled. 'You know what Tagore's trouble is? No, of course you don't, so I'll tell you. I won some money off him at cards once when we were both in Colombo. Had the devil of a time recovering it. He didn't like it when I put the word around to make sure he didn't get the chance to cheat anyone else. He'd be happy to lay any trumped-up charge at my door to discredit me.'

Tagore didn't look like a gambler, reflected de Silva, but he didn't have the evidence to dismiss Renshaw's claim. The man had him foiled and he knew it. Still, he mustn't give in too readily.

'All the same, with your permission, I'd like to visit the labour lines.'

Renshaw came around to de Silva's side of the desk and brought his face very close. 'My workers are as well treated as any in the area, Inspector. If you persist in harassing me by suggesting otherwise, I'll take a complaint of my own to the assistant government agent. This plantation is my property. I won't tolerate anyone poking around stirring up my workforce. Now, if you'll excuse me, I have work to do.'

He opened the door; the fingers of one hand drummed on the wood. 'Good afternoon, Inspector.'

De Silva felt angry with the assistant government agent, with Tagore, and also with himself. Renshaw was obnoxious but he was no fool and he, de Silva, should have anticipated that. This had all the hallmarks of a fruitless investigation, but he couldn't shirk it now. His next move must be to apply for a warrant to search the labour lines and interview Renshaw's workers.

Yet even that would be of doubtful use. If this man

Gooptu was alive, it was unlikely he would be there, and even more unlikely that the other workers would be willing to risk their jobs by speaking out.

He had one more try at Renshaw. 'If you have nothing to hide, sir, I suggest you reconsider and save us both a lot of trouble. As I expect you're aware, I can apply for a warrant.'

'That's up to you, Inspector. But I assure you, you'll be wasting your time. I dismissed Gooptu. He packed his bag and left. That's all there is to it.'

He held the door a little wider and after a moment's hesitation, de Silva nodded curtly and walked out of the room. Downstairs, he emerged into the sunshine as a black Daimler drew up outside the factory.

The man who got out of the driving seat had jet-black hair that contrasted sharply with his pale complexion. From his colouring and the oval shape of his eyes, de Silva guessed he was Eurasian. The man noticed him and stared for a moment before giving a brief nod and striding into the factory. The penetrating look reminded de Silva of a photograph of an Arctic wolf he had once seen in a magazine.

He started back down the dirt road to where he had left the Morris. When he opened the driver's door, a wave of trapped, boiling air rolled out. The tan leather seat was searing to the touch. He wound back the hood and was about to ease himself in when he noticed a sandy-haired boy of six or seven watching him from a few yards inside the gates to the plantation bungalow. De Silva smiled and received a shy smile in return.

'I like your car, sir.'

'Thank you.'

'Does it go very fast?'

'Pretty fast, nearly fifty miles an hour. Come and have a better look if you like.'

The boy came forward until he was close enough to

touch the car. Tentatively, he put out a small, freckled hand and stroked the gleaming navy paintwork.

'Hamish!'

They both swung around. A slight young woman with fair hair hurried across the grass.

'Hamish, what are you doing out here? You know you're not to leave the garden by yourself. Where's your ayah?'

A rebellious look came over Hamish's face. He balled his fists. 'I don't want her with me all the time. I'm not a baby.'

The woman sighed. 'No, you're not a baby, so you're old enough to do as you're told.' She looked at de Silva and he saw her eyes dwell briefly on his police badge. 'Good afternoon. I hope my son wasn't making a nuisance of himself.'

'Not at all, ma'am. We were just talking about the car.'

She smiled. 'Yes, Hamish loves cars, and we're rather off the beaten track here. Not many come this way.'

'But there've been two today,' Hamish piped up. 'This one and the big black one.'

De Silva noticed the woman's smile vanish abruptly. Clearly, she was not keen on her husband's visitor.

'May I introduce myself?' he asked. 'Inspector Shanti de Silva.' He gave a little bow. There was a defenceless air to this woman that seemed to require a reassuring display of old-fashioned gallantry.

She held out a delicate white hand. 'I'm Madeleine Renshaw. Have you been up to visit my husband? I hope there's nothing wrong.'

The artless way she said it made him think that she had no idea about the flogging business.

'Nothing at all, ma'am. It was merely a routine visit.'

There was a pause. 'I believe you know my wife,' he said.

A glimmer of surprise lit Madeleine Renshaw's eyes then was extinguished. 'Oh, of course I do. We both attend St George's church in town. She welcomed me very kindly when I arrived, but I'm afraid I don't have much time to join in local activities. We only moved here from Colombo a short while ago and there's so much to do.' Her voice held a trace of defensiveness.

'I'm sorry to hear it. Perhaps when you're more settled? I'm sure my wife would be delighted to help.'

'Perhaps. Well, I mustn't keep you from your duties, Inspector.'

Hamish tugged at his mother's skirt. 'Can I show him Jacko?'

'Not today, darling. The inspector has more important matters to attend to.'

'Pleease?'

De Silva smiled. 'And who is Jacko?'

'My bird. I'm teaching him to talk.'

'Ah, is he a mynah bird?'

Hamish nodded eagerly. 'He's very clever.'

'I'm sure he is. I had one when I was about your age. It learnt to say many things. They are excellent mimics.'

'Pleease, Mamma?'

'Oh, very well. Can you spare the time, Inspector?'

De Silva deliberated for a beat. He doubted Charles Renshaw would be pleased to find that he was still on his property, but it might be worth furthering an acquaintance with his wife. Renshaw had mentioned getting a shipment ready for tomorrow so it was a fairly safe bet he wouldn't come down from the factory until lunchtime at least. He nodded. 'It will be a pleasure.'

'Would you like to bring your car into the driveway?'

'Thank you.'

Hamish beamed. 'Can I sit in the passenger seat?'

De Silva laughed. 'Of course, if your mother has no objection.'

'You don't, do you, Mamma?' asked the little boy quickly, already scampering to the passenger side of the Morris. He jumped in and started to examine the instruments on the walnut dashboard.

His mother shook her head. 'I'm afraid his manners leave something to be desired, Inspector. I'll see you on the verandah.'

De Silva went slowly up to the bungalow, glancing once or twice at Madeleine Renshaw as she took a short cut across the lawn. Her figure was slender, and she walked gracefully.

By the time he and Hamish reached the verandah, she was sitting in one of four rattan chairs arranged around a table with a blue cloth. An unchecked jasmine rambled over the tiled roof, shading the seating area, and spilling its perfume into the air.

'I've told the servant to bring us iced tea, Inspector. I hope that will suit you.'

De Silva thanked her then gave an involuntary start as a black shape swooped onto the back of one of the rattan chairs. 'Ah, I expect this is Jacko.'

The mynah bird shuffled sideways along the chair rail and cocked its head. 'Hello? Tea, mangoes?' It followed its remarks with a raucous burst of shrieks and whistles.

Madeleine Renshaw winced. 'I'm sorry, Inspector.'

'There's no need to apologise. My bird was just as noisy.'

'What did you call him?' asked Hamish.

'Rascal, because my mother said that was the best name for him. I'm afraid he eventually disgraced himself by using bad language and she banished him to the servants' quarters. I had to play with him there.'

'What's bad language?'

'Something you're too young to know about yet,' his mother said firmly. 'Ah, here's the tea.'

The servant set a tray of iced tea and small cakes on the table then flapped his hands at the mynah bird. With a volley of indignant squawks, it flew up to perch on a corner of the roof where it stayed, watching the cakes with beady eyes.

'You must find life very different here from Colombo,' said de Silva, making conversation as he put one of the cakes Madeleine Renshaw offered him onto his plate. He took a bite. The sponge was heavier than the cakes their cook made at home.

'I do. Colombo was always so hot and busy. I never liked it much. It's much more beautiful here and the air is better for Hamish. I worried about his health in Colombo.'

Hamish had taken his cake and was crouching on the lawn where he had enticed Jacko down from his perch with a scattering of crumbs.

'He has far fewer coughs now,' Madeleine went on.

'Has he lived out in Ceylon all his life?'

She shook her head. 'He was born in England, but he doesn't remember it. He was only ten months old when his father and I brought him to the island.'

'It must have been hard coping with such a young child in a strange country. Did you and Mr Renshaw already know people out here?'

'Oh, Charles isn't Hamish's father. Hamish is my son by my first husband.' Her face clouded. 'He fell ill and died when Hamish was three years old. Not long after that I met Charles. He was very kind and—'

Jacko suddenly landed in the middle of the table, rocking plates and cups.

'Oh, this wretched bird!' Madeleine flapped her hands. A flush sprang to her cheeks. Jacko shrieked and took off again. He landed on the lawn and strutted up and down, his feathers ruffled. 'Get out, get out! Mangoes!' he squawked.

'Hamish! Take your bird away *now*, or like Inspector de Silva's mother, I will banish him for good.'

Hamish scrambled to his feet. 'Sorry, Mamma.' He ran off across the lawn, leaving a trail of crumbs for the bird to follow.

'I suppose Jacko is less trouble than a dog,' Madeleine said ruefully.

The blast of a siren sounded from the direction of the factory. Her head jerked around. 'They're finishing work for the morning. I'd offer you lunch, Inspector, but my husband is always in such a hurry.'

De Silva stood up. 'I wouldn't dream of imposing on you, ma'am. Although it would be a great pleasure to spend longer in your company, I must be getting back to the station.'

He waved to Hamish. 'Goodbye! Be careful what you teach your bird.'

Negotiating the rutted road back to Nuala, de Silva pondered over the little encounter. When she relaxed and the pinched, careworn expression left her face, Madeleine Renshaw was a pretty woman. It was easy to see how a certain sort of man would want to protect her, but Renshaw didn't seem that kind, in fact more of a brute.

There must be a good fifteen years between them in age. He wondered what they had in common. Their marriage certainly seemed an unlikely love match. But then he was no expert in such matters. It was taxing enough to fathom the schemes and mysteries of the human mind, let alone the human heart.

His mind turned to the warrant he needed to apply for if he was to question the workers at Renshaw's labour lines. Clutterbuck was the appropriate man to hear the application; among his numerous duties, he served as the magistrate for the Nuala area.

De Silva sighed. Clutterbuck was unlikely to be happy about granting it, but there was no help for that and when all was said and done, he was a fair-minded man. He'd better telephone from the station to make an appointment to see him and explain the situation.

At the station, the smell of curry greeted him. Sergeant

Prasanna and Constable Nadar were having lunch. Prasanna wiped a smear of dahl from his chin as they both jumped to attention. 'Good afternoon, sir,' they chorused.

'It's alright, get on with your meal.'

De Silva looked at the assortment of tin containers and plates on Prasanna's desk. 'Your mother's famous coconut roti, eh? A secret recipe, I believe?'

'Yes, sir.' Prasanna grinned. 'She wants to feed me up for the match on Saturday.'

'Then victory is assured. But maybe you should put in some practice as well, just to be absolutely certain. If there's nothing urgent you may take the afternoon off. Constable Nadar will be happy to hold the fort, I'm sure.'

The sergeant's face brightened. 'Thank you, sir.'

'Nadar, I have a telephone call to make, then if you need me, I'll be at home.'

The chubby constable looked disconsolate. 'Yes, sir.'

In his office de Silva made the call to the Residence. To his relief, he found he had a temporary respite. Archie Clutterbuck had gone on an expedition to Horton Plains.

* * *

The early afternoon sun beat down on the garden at Sunny-bank; the roses drooped. A fat spotted dove pecked in the flowerbeds, hunting for worms and insects. A pair of green bee-eaters chirruped among the leaves of the plantain tree.

Indoors all was silent but one of the house servants soon appeared.

'Where's the memsahib?' asked de Silva.

'At her ladies' sewing circle, sahib.'

'Of course, I'd forgotten it's today. I want some lunch. What do we have in the kitchen?'

'Vegetables in coconut milk, brinjal and curried cashew with peas.'

'Good, bring me some of all of them and some rice. I'll eat on the verandah.'

Half an hour later, he sat in the shade enjoying his food with liberal seasonings of lime pickle and chutney. The brinjal was delicious. It surprised him that, according to Jane, no one ate eggplant in England. Such a tasty vegetable and so healthy. But the English had strange ideas about food. Most of the English dishes he had eaten had seemed to him bland and overcooked.

When he had eaten his fill and the dishes were cleared away, he leant back in his chair and let his gaze wander over the garden. It was wonderful the way that contemplating it made the troubles of the day dwindle to insignificance. He would decide what to say to Tagore and Archie Clutterbuck tomorrow. For now, he wanted a nap.

The air had cooled, and the sun was slipping behind the trees when Jane woke him with a tap on his shoulder. She smiled. 'A busy day, dear?'

He shook himself and stretched. 'Thinking is a very tiring activity.'

'And what were you thinking about?'

'How to deal with this business up at the Renshaw plantation.'

'Have you seen him?'

'Yes, I went up earlier today. He didn't admit to flogging this man Gooptu, and I wasn't able to find out his side of the story.'

'Why not?'

'Renshaw said he'd dismissed him and didn't know where he'd gone.'

'Did you believe him?'

De Silva shrugged. 'I'm not sure. Renshaw's a thoroughly unpleasant character. I wouldn't put it past him to ill-treat his workers but without seeing this man Gooptu, I've nothing more to go on than Tagore's allegations. I asked Renshaw if I could go down to his labour lines and speak to some of his people, but he flatly refused. He said if the police persisted in harassing him, he'd take a complaint of his own to Archie Clutterbuck.'

'Did you tell him who made the complaint?'

'I didn't need to. He'd worked that out for himself. He knew Tagore was in town.'

'So what will you do?'

'I'll have to apply to Archie Clutterbuck for a warrant.'

'Does he know you want one?'

'Not yet. I telephoned the Residence, but he was up at Horton Plains on a fishing expedition and not back until tomorrow evening.'

'And what about Tagore?'

'He can wait; he's made enough mischief already.'

'Shanti!'

'I'm sorry. I'm prepared to stick my neck out and apply for this warrant, but I don't have much confidence I'll find anything to support a charge against Renshaw. Your Mr Tagore may have embroiled me in trouble with the British for nothing.'

'It's always worth standing up to injustice, Shanti.'

He put his arm around her. 'The voice of my conscience. I'm doing all I can, my dear, but I won't get results without good evidence.'

'Bullies like Renshaw make me so angry. He's one of the worst sorts of plantation owners.'

'I know, and one day they will have to change or lose everything. But I'm afraid that day may still be a long way off.'

That evening after dinner they sat in the drawing room by the fire. The Tiffany lamp on the table at Jane's side cast bronze and rose-pink light over her face as she turned the pages of her book. He watched her for a while, regretting that the silence between them didn't seem to have its usual companionable air, but perhaps it was better not to reopen the discussion about Renshaw tonight. In any case, what more could he say? He didn't want to mention the blood-stained shirt. She would be distressed by the thought of it and even more so if it led her to question whether Gooptu had been not just flogged but killed.

She looked up. 'Is *Ivanhoe* still proving tiresome?'

'Perhaps I've read too much of Sir Walter's work. His style begins to feel a little stale.'

'You should read Mrs Christie. She's far more entertaining.'

'But that would be too much of a – what's the English expression – a bus driver's holiday?'

'A bus*man*'s holiday, dear.'

'I forgot to ask if you had a pleasant afternoon at your sewing circle.'

'Very pleasant, thank you.'

'Who was there?'

'Oh, the usual people, you know. The vicar's wife, some of the planters' wives, and of course Florence Clutterbuck. She's in charge of the project to replace the church kneelers. As she would be.'

De Silva chuckled. 'Of course. I hope you behaved nicely.'

'When have I ever done otherwise? We had a very amicable chat about all kinds of things.'

'Good. I'm glad to hear the claws were sheathed.'

Jane sniffed and returned to her book.

He stood up and went over to kiss her. 'I was only teasing.'

She smiled. 'I know.'

'I'm going to take a turn around the garden before bed.'

'In the dark?'

He pointed to the window. 'No, the moon is very bright this evening. There'll be plenty of light to see by.'

'Well, wrap up. It will be cold out there.'

After the warmth inside, the air was like a draught of cool water. He exhaled and his breath turned into a little cloud. The moonlight cast an otherworldly glow over the garden. Small creatures rustled and scampered in the undergrowth and an owl hooted. From far away he heard a series of faint bangs. That would be the firecrackers that the local farmers set off to scare away wild elephants and prevent them from destroying the crops.

He crossed the lawn to the flowerbeds where his roses grew and admired the blooms. Some of them were smaller than the length of his thumb, others the size of a small dinner plate. Nearby, some dahlias grew. He fingered the thick, fleshy stem of one of the tallest plants. It reached almost to his shoulder. He had read somewhere that there were countries where the dahlia's hollow stems were dried and used as pipes to enable swimmers to breathe underwater.

The moonlight glimmered on the pearly shell of a snail inching its way along a leaf. He picked it off and its soft, slimy body retracted swiftly. Maybe it was the moonlight that made him whimsical, but it suddenly seemed like a symbol of Ceylon's progress to independence, creeping forwards then recoiling when faced with overwhelming odds.

He took the snail over to a pile of dead leaves and placed it gently on top. Even though he rarely visited the temple nowadays, his Buddhist upbringing still made him loath to take away life without good reason.

His brow furrowed. Why wasn't he as angry as Jane about this Renshaw business? It was too easy to dismiss her views as womanly emotion. If a snail was important, wasn't a man even more so? Yes, but the rule of law was important too and he cared deeply about that. It was one of the reasons he had joined the police force in the first place. Men like Renshaw must be overcome by legal means, not the court of public opinion, and if that took time, the maintenance of law and order justified the wait.

Poor Ceylon! His country had known so many foreign conquerors: first the kings and princes of Southern India, then the Portuguese, the Dutch and finally, the British. But life for many people under the British was not so bad. They had built schools, roads, and railways; tarmac and iron had sliced a way through virgin jungle, climbed rolling hills and opened the way to the palm-fringed beaches of the Indian Ocean. The British had brought tea bushes and rubber trees. Would Ceylon really be better off if she tried to stand on her own feet now? He loved his country as much as any man and wanted her to be free one day, but he feared what might happen if independence from the British came too soon. Ceylon had had many names – the Teardrop of India, the Pearl of the Indian Ocean, the Paradise Island. But paradise was a fragile construction.

When he and Jane were first married, he had read the Christian bible to try and understand her faith better. The story of Adam and Eve that it contained taught how easily paradise could be lost. Gooptu might have suffered an injustice but what mattered was the greater good. Patience was better than bloodshed.

The snail disappeared into the pile of leaves, leaving only a silver trail behind. 'Wise creature,' de Silva murmured. 'You know how to bide your time.'

CHAPTER 7

De Silva and Jane ate breakfast in the dining room the following morning. She had decreed it too chilly to sit on the verandah. He held out his cup and she poured him more tea. He added milk and three generous spoons of sugar then looked up. 'What's the matter?'

'Shanti dear, think of your waistline.'

He patted his middle. 'What of it?'

'It's expanding.'

'Next you'll be wanting me to take exercise.'

She laughed. 'Well, a little exercise wouldn't hurt.'

'I'll tell you what, give me a couple of hours to go to the station then we can have that picnic at the lake after all. I'll take you out for a row in one of the boats. Will that satisfy you?'

'Lovely. I'll tell cook to make sandwiches. I think there's some cake left from yesterday.'

'Sandwiches?'

'This is going to be an English picnic, dear. It will make a nice change.'

'If you say so.'

He drank the last of his tea and put down the cup. 'I suppose it's time I was off.'

Jane got up from her chair, came over to his side of the table and planted a big kiss on his cheek.

'What do I deserve that for?'

'I'm very proud of you, Shanti. You do know it, don't you? I hope our conversation yesterday didn't make you think otherwise. I know I mustn't assume this man Renshaw is guilty just because I dislike the sound of him.'

He kissed her back. 'And I mustn't take it for granted that because something is difficult, it's not worth pursuing. It's good for me to be reminded that I must stick to my rifles.'

'Stick to your guns, dear. It's stick to your guns.'

Before he left for the station, de Silva went to inspect his garden. He was glad to find that apart from a few browned leaves and fallen petals, the roses seemed none the worse for the cold night.

The Morris's engine purred into life, and he kept up a good speed until he was nearly at the police station when he came upon a bullock cart with a broken axle blocking one side of the road. A horde of rickshaws trying to get past it had ground to a halt in a cacophony of horn blowing and imprecations. Constable Nadar's rotund figure was in the midst of it all, his earnest face glowing with exertion as he tried to untangle the mess.

De Silva leant back in his seat and tapped his fingers on the walnut steering wheel. Poor Nadar. He was a nice young man and very willing, but his organisational skills left something to be desired.

The driver of the cart finally succeeded in unharnessing the two massive-shouldered beasts and led them away while other men unloaded sacks and bales from the cart and manhandled it to the side of the road. De Silva gently pressed his foot on the accelerator and eased the Morris forward. The crowd of rickshaws and bystanders parted before him. As he cleared the jam and the Morris speeded up, he saw a black Daimler approach from the direction of the road that led to the Five Palms plantation. The man de Silva had seen at the plantation was at the wheel with

Charles Renshaw in the passenger seat. Renshaw saw the Morris and immediately averted his gaze.

The Daimler went by too fast for de Silva to make out any passengers in the back. He shrugged and drove on to the station where Sergeant Prasanna jumped to his feet. 'Good morning, sir.'

De Silva tossed his hat onto the hat stand and nodded. 'I see Nadar is on traffic duty this morning.'

'Yes, sir. I thought I'd better hold the fort here.'

'Any calls?'

'No, sir.'

'So, what have we on today? Have you made any progress with that break-in at the Ayurvedic shop?'

'I'm afraid not. That street is very quiet at night. There are only a few people living there and none of them heard anything.'

'But you said the owner reported that nothing of any importance seemed to have been stolen.'

'That's right.'

'Well, I suggest you tell him there's no more we can do for the moment. Find out how much it will cost to repair his locks and tell him he'll be given some compensation from the police fund. That should satisfy him.'

'Very well, sir.'

'You look glum, Sergeant. Is there something else?'

Prasanna sighed. 'It's my mother, sir. It turns out she knows Doctor Bandi – he's the owner. She gets her wrinkle creams and her tonics from him. The long and the short of it is he'll complain to her that I haven't found the culprits and she'll keep telling me off about it.'

De Silva had met the sergeant's mother, a formidable widow who owned a beauty shop. She barely reached to her only son's shoulder, yet she ruled him with an iron rod. Prasanna had obviously inherited his good looks from her, but his easy-going nature must have come from his father.

'The worst of it is,' Prasanna went on gloomily, 'when she's annoyed about something, she always comes back to the same subject.'

'And that is?'

'She complains that I do not marry.'

'Ah.' De Silva remembered his own mother's views on the subject of his marriage prospects. He had spent many years trying to explain why he didn't want to marry any of the suitable girls she found for him. His father had simply rolled his eyes and disappeared to his vegetable patch until the storm blew over.

'It's worst of all when she sees Constable Nadar's mother at the bazaar. She's always talking, talking, talking about her lovely daughter-in-law and her beautiful grandchild. My mother says I have no heart and why am I being so stubborn when Nadar is two years younger than me and a family man already?'

De Silva cleared his throat and gave Prasanna what he intended to be a fatherly pat on the shoulder. 'If you'll take my advice, young man, you'll stand up to your mother and wait for a woman you love to come along. I did and I've always been very glad of it.'

Prasanna looked dubious but he nodded. 'Thank you for your good advice, sir.'

The door opened and a perspiring Nadar came in.

'All in order, Constable?'

Nadar nodded. 'I'm sorry you were kept waiting, sir.'

'Never mind. If you're all done, bring my tea to my office, will you?'

'Yes, sir.'

In his office he wrote a brief report of his visit to the Five Palms plantation then set down his pen and contemplated the opposite wall for a few moments. His hand hovered to the telephone, and he picked up the receiver and dialled. The operator's voice came on the line with that peculiarly hollow sound that made it seem as if she was speaking from the bottom of a well. He gave the number of the Nuala Hotel. After two rings a polite voice answered. De Silva asked for Tagore and then waited.

A few moments later, the voice came back on the line. 'Mr Tagore is staying at the hotel, sir, but he appears to be out. May I take a message?'

'Please tell him Inspector de Silva called. I shall be out myself for the rest of the day, but he can reach me at the police station on Monday.'

'Certainly, Inspector.'

He put down the receiver. There, that was done. He picked up the copy of *The Colombo Times* that lay neatly folded on his desk. The paper crackled as he opened it and scanned the articles. There were still shortages of rice due to the drought; an Australian cricket team was visiting Colombo. A full-page article showed the members of the Black Lotus gang. It listed their sentences and praised the dedication of the Colombo police in rounding them up. A short paragraph near the bottom of the page mentioned his name. He stood up and tucked the paper under his arm. Jane might like to see the article, small as his part in it was.

* * *

The morning chill had vanished, but a light breeze ruffled the aquamarine surface of the lake making the temperature of the air pleasantly cool. As they walked across the grass to find a good picnic spot, a couple of shaggy brown ponies trotted over to them.

'Are they some of the strays you mentioned?' Jane asked.

'Yes, Prasanna still hasn't found out who owns them.' He flapped his hands to send them away, but the ponies stood their ground.

'Poor creatures,' said Jane. 'I suppose they have water and grass here, but they really should be looked after properly.' A pensive look came into her eyes. 'We might have space for one of them at least.'

De Silva thought of his roses, and she laughed. 'I was only teasing, dear. No need to look so horrified. But seriously, something ought to be done.'

'I know, and I have Prasanna on it, but I'm afraid his mind is more occupied with cricket at the moment. After the match is over, I shall press him harder.'

One of the ponies came close, flicking its tail and whickering gently, then suddenly it shied as with a loud caw a crow landed close by. The pony wheeled and trotted away in the direction of the water, followed by its companions.

'That's better.' De Silva spread the picnic rug out on the grass and put down the hamper. As Jane unpacked it, he surveyed the lake. A flotilla of small rowing boats bobbed at anchor by a jetty. Two had already been taken out but there were plenty left for them to get one after lunch.

He turned back to his wife. 'What have we got?'

She opened a box and produced the sandwiches. 'Egg and cress, sardines, and pork luncheon meat. And I had cook put in some butter cake for you.'

'You're too good to me,' he said with a grin.

He picked up a sardine sandwich and took a bite. He would never fathom why the British liked their food so bland.

As they ate, and drank Elephant ginger beer, they chatted and watched all the other people enjoying an afternoon by the lake. A large Ceylonese family were picnicking nearby, the women dressed in a rainbow of saris and chattering like a flock of Brahminy starlings. The men wore the ubiquitous sarongs and shirts and were quieter, either talking in pairs or simply lounging while they smoked and gazed out over the lake. A gaggle of children played on the shoreline, running in and out of the water with squeals of excitement and scooping up handfuls of it to throw at each other. The hardier ones had ventured in up to their necks and were swimming about, their dark hair gleaming.

Jane smiled. 'It's lovely to see them having such fun.' She looked more closely at the children playing. Amongst the crowd of lithe dark bodies was one that was pale and hanging back from the rest.

She shaded her eyes with her hand. 'Poor little mite,' she said. 'He must be shy.'

De Silva followed her gaze. 'Why, it's the Renshaw boy, Hamish.' He scanned the bank. 'And Madeleine Renshaw over by the kiosk watching him.'

'It wouldn't do for Florence Clutterbuck to see her,' Jane remarked. 'She wouldn't approve of her letting her son play with "the natives" as Florence likes to call them.'

De Silva shrugged. He tried to regard the assistant government agent's wife as an amusing curiosity and not let her ignorant remarks trouble him. She wasn't the only Britisher to use the term "natives": a description that belittled his country's ancient and rich civilization. Many didn't bother to understand what a melting pot his country was. First the Sinhalese, his own people – the original inhabitants of Ceylon – then the Tamils, either coming in over the centuries in waves of invasion from South India or brought to Ceylon more recently by the British to pick the tea.

'Shanti?'

'What? Oh, Hamish. He won't come to any harm. Tucked away at that plantation, I expect the poor lad gets precious little chance to meet playmates his own age.'

'I'm sure you're right.'

'At least he has his bird.'

'His bird?'

'It's a mynah. He's teaching it to talk. It's an impudent little creature.'

'Then it had better not be introduced to Florence.'

De Silva finished his sardine sandwich and helped himself to an egg and cress. Ceylon's version of Buddhism didn't require its followers to be strict vegetarians and he sometimes ate meat; luncheon meat was, however, a step too far. In his opinion, it was one of the least appealing of British creations.

'That would be unwise, I agree,' he replied. 'It might be executed for high treason.'

Jane shaded her eyes again. 'That's a very pretty dress she has on – Madeleine Renshaw, I mean. And my gracious, if I'm not very much mistaken, that's Ravindra Tagore coming over to talk to her. I wonder how they know each other. Perhaps they met in Colombo. She's never mentioned him but then again there's been no reason why she should. Do you want to go over and speak to them?'

'No. I'm not on duty. Monday is quite soon enough to tackle Mr Tagore, and I haven't anything to say to Renshaw's wife.'

Jane pursed her lips. 'Very well,' she said stiffly. 'I just thought it might be a good opportunity.'

A twinge of contrition for his grumpiness came over him. It must be envy of the delightful aromas of coriander, cumin, chilli, and ginger that were floating across from the Ceylonese family party. Their servants were busy unpacking dozens of tin boxes and pails of food and heating it on a collection of primus stoves they had set up. With a sigh, he selected another egg sandwich.

'Anyway,' he mumbled through a mouthful. 'I know you too well. You're just curious to find out how they know each other and it's really none of our business.'

Jane laughed. 'I suppose that's true. But seriously, I'm certain her husband wouldn't like it.'

They had finished the sandwiches when a fruit seller came past. De Silva stopped him and bought slices of fresh pineapple and mango chunks seasoned with chilli and lime. He popped a large chunk of mango in his mouth and savoured it. A dribble of saffron juice ran down his chin. Jane handed him a napkin. 'Mop your chin, dear.'

Once the fruit was finished, he stood up. 'Well, are you ready to go for this row?'

'If you are, dear.'

She glanced in the direction of the kiosk. 'Ah, Mr Tagore seems to have gone, but you'll have to find something to say to Mrs Renshaw after all. She and her son are coming this way. Maybe we shouldn't mention we've already seen them. She might think it unfriendly of me not to have gone over to say hello before. What a pity. It will have to be a mystery how she knows Ravindra Tagore.'

She beamed. 'Why, Mrs Renshaw! What a nice surprise, and this must be your little boy. Have you been swimming, my dear? I hope it wasn't too cold?'

Madeleine Renshaw's fair hair was neat, but she raised a hand to brush an imaginary strand back from her face. As he greeted her, de Silva noticed that the hand trembled and a flush reddened her slim neck. 'Mrs de Silva… Inspector. What a pleasure to see you.'

De Silva didn't believe that for a moment.

'Are you just in town for the day?' asked Jane.

'Charles and Hamish and I are staying at the Crown tonight. Charles has some business here today and we plan to come to the cricket tomorrow.'

Jane smiled at Hamish who was hanging back. 'My husband tells me you have a very clever bird,' she said.

Hamish nodded shyly. 'He's called Jacko. He can say forty words already and I'm going to teach him lots more.'

'How wonderful. I hope I can meet him one day.'

'I wanted a dog, but Mamma said I couldn't have one, but now I think Jacko's better.'

'I'm afraid my husband dislikes dogs,' said Madeleine.

There was a pause. 'Well, it was very nice to see you,' she said awkwardly.

'Likewise. I expect we'll meet again at the cricket tomorrow.' Jane lowered her voice. 'We have high hopes of Shanti's sergeant. We call him Nuala's secret weapon.'

'There,' Jane whispered as Madeleine Renshaw and her son walked away. 'That wasn't so hard, was it? She's a perfectly pleasant woman. I feel sorry for her with that husband of hers.'

They packed away the remains of the picnic and de Silva stowed the hamper in the Morris's trunk. Down at the lakeshore, he paid the boatman for an hour's hire and he and Jane were soon out on the water. Rowing was harder work than it looked, he thought, as he pulled on the oars, trying to dip them in the water without splashing. Jane sat back on the cushioned seat opposite him, holding her blue parasol over her head for shade.

'This is really very pleasant,' she said with a smile.

'Good. I'm glad you're enjoying it.'

A gaggle of pygmy geese landed nearby and honked around in a circle, their heads bobbing. 'Hoping for bread, I expect,' said Jane. 'What pretty little birds they are with that black and white plumage and their bright eyes.'

'I'm afraid they're out of luck.'

They lapsed into silence and de Silva's thoughts drifted back to Madeleine Renshaw. If it had been Tagore she was talking with, did she know about his feud with her husband? Surely if she did, she would avoid the fellow. Or if she knew Tagore from her old life, might she have some idea she could influence him to drop his complaint?

He looked at the sun. Their hour must be almost up.

'Shall we start back?' asked Jane.

'I suppose we should.'

'If you don't mind, I'd like to stop at St George's on

the way home. I want to see the kneelers that have been completed. We needn't stay long.'

'Very well.'

* * *

The church was cool inside; the dark wood of the beamed roof gleamed richly against the white of the walls. In the apse the late afternoon sun made the stained-glass windows glow with intensity, but the recessed windows flanking the nave were glazed with plain glass letting in plenty of light.

De Silva sat in one of the pews while Jane walked around studying the new kneelers and occasionally holding one up for him to admire.

When he had proposed to her and she accepted, he had soon realised that she would be deeply disappointed if their marriage was not recognised by her church. He came to the conclusion that it would not be impossible to accommodate his Buddhist philosophy with Christianity. He had never discussed this view outright with the vicar who conducted the service of blessing after the civil ceremony, but the man had the air of being someone who understood that the human spirit need not, necessarily, be confined by one creed. Man is capable of worshipping in many ways.

In any case, he had come to find his visits to this church very soothing. He enjoyed singing the hymns and the vicar kept his sermons short. However, he still preferred the profusion of flowers in the Buddhist temple; the stiff arrangements favoured by Florence Clutterbuck and her entourage weren't quite the same. He also loved the aromas that intoxicated the senses and the tom-toms that set your blood racing, so he continued to go to the temple when he felt the need. He was pleased that on occasion, Jane came with him.

The entrance door to the church creaked and he turned to see a wedge of lemon light fall across the floor. To his surprise, the man who came in was Ravindra Tagore. He seemed preoccupied and at first gave no sign of noticing that he wasn't alone.

A circular metal stand for candles stood under one of the aisle windows. Tagore went over to it, put some money in the box underneath, and took a candle. He touched the wick to one that was already alight and put his candle in one of the sconces. For a few moments he stood with his head bowed.

De Silva was tempted to wait and see if he would leave afterwards. If so, he could avoid having to acknowledge him, but as Tagore finished his moment of silent contemplation, Jane noticed him. 'Why, Mr Tagore,' she said warmly. 'Do you remember me? I was governess to the Macfarlane family in Colombo at one time. You used to visit their home quite often.'

De Silva edged to the end of his pew, hoping she wouldn't engage Tagore in conversation for too long. Briefly, he looked confused then his face cleared. 'Miss Hart! Of course I remember you. Is your home in Nuala now?'

'Yes, my husband and I have lived here for some time.'

'Ah, I had no idea you were married. My felicitations.'

'Thank you. So what brings you to our little town, Mr Tagore?'

'My mother's death. My father died many years ago and I was their only child, so it is my duty to settle her affairs.'

'I'm so sorry. It's always a sad business when a parent dies.'

He nodded. 'But she was very frail in the last few years. Life had become a burden she no longer relished.'

'Is she buried in the churchyard here?'

'Yes. She was a Christian as was my father. I do not have their faith,' he added.

'Yet you light a candle for your mother. I'm sure that would have made her happy.'

He shrugged. 'I hope so. I'm afraid I wasn't always the most attentive of sons.' There was a pause. 'Well,' he resumed, 'it's a pleasure to see you again, but if you'll excuse me…'

'Of course, I'm sure you have a great deal to do. I was on the point of leaving myself.'

'May I escort you somewhere?'

'Thank you, but there's no need. My husband is with me.' She gestured to the pew where de Silva sat, and Tagore stiffened. Wishing that Jane had not embroiled him in this meeting, de Silva stood up. He might as well be civil to the man. Snubbing him was likely to make him harder to deal with.

He extended a hand. 'Good afternoon, Mr Tagore. I telephoned your hotel this morning and they told me you were out. I left a message saying I would be back at the police station on Monday if you wished to speak to me.'

Tagore flushed slightly. 'That won't be necessary now, Inspector. I return to Colombo in the morning. As you indicated, the matter we discussed needs to be dealt with in the proper manner. I feel I've done my part by reporting it to you. From henceforward I'm content to rely on your judgement.'

De Silva frowned. This was a turn up for the book, as the British said. What had happened to the zealous young firebrand who confronted him yesterday?

'Oh, what a pity you have to go,' said Jane, breaking the silence. 'We have our annual cricket match against Hatton tomorrow. Couldn't you spare another day? There must be a lot of people who would like to see you before you leave.'

Tagore shook his head. 'Apart from yourself, Mrs de Silva, I have no friends in Nuala. I visited infrequently when my mother was alive and then only to spend time with her.'

'He looks troubled,' said Jane as the door of the church closed after Tagore. 'Don't you think it's odd he didn't mention knowing Madeleine Renshaw? And he doesn't appear to be much bothered about Gooptu now. That's a real change of tune since yesterday, isn't it?'

De Silva wasn't sure what to think. This was an unexpected development; a strange one too when Tagore had so recently seemed passionate about the matter. And now he, de Silva, was saddled with this application for a warrant and the prospect of explaining himself to the assistant government agent. Had he been right about Madeleine Renshaw's intervention? If so, she was a wilier creature than he'd thought.

He took his wife's arm. 'Odd, I agree, but don't start reading too much into it, my dear. It won't stop me pursuing the investigation either. Now, if you've finished here, shall we go home?'

CHAPTER 8

Saturday dawned clear and bright. As de Silva waited in the garden for Jane to come out, he breathed in the perfume of the rambling rose that smothered the trellis separating the garden from the driveway.

'Here I am.' Jane smiled as she twirled to show off her new dress – a navy silk with white polka dots. A navy picture hat with a matching trim and wrist-length white gloves completed the outfit.

He kissed her cheek. 'You look very charming.'

'Thank you, dear. You look very smart too.'

When he wasn't in uniform, de Silva often wore Ceylonese dress for comfort, but today he had chosen west-ern-style clothes – cream trousers, a lightweight navy blazer and a white shirt. He offered her his arm. 'Shall we go?'

The Morris purred down the drive and headed in the direction of the cricket ground. A lot of people had already arrived, and the refreshment tents and stalls were busy. They moved through the crowd for a while, pausing to greet friends and acquaintances, then Jane tugged his sleeve. 'Here come the Clutterbucks.'

De Silva chuckled. 'You must think of something nice to say to Florence.'

'So must you.'

Florence Clutterbuck sailed towards them. Her ample figure was encased in a flowery dress topped off by a hat in a shade of fuchsia pink that fought with her flushed cheeks. 'Good morning,' she fluted. 'Such a beautiful day, isn't it?'

De Silva smiled. 'Indeed it is, ma'am. And even better if we win the match.'

'Absolutely.' Archie Clutterbuck joined them. He too looked hot in a linen suit and Panama hat. De Silva recognised the MCC tie. Clutterbuck bowed to Jane. 'What a pleasure to see you, Mrs de Silva.'

They talked for a few moments then de Silva found that Clutterbuck had contrived to edge him out of earshot of the ladies. 'Any progress with the Renshaw business?' he asked quietly.

De Silva took a deep breath. This was a conversation he would rather not have today. He would eventually have to disclose that Tagore had backed off, but that left him in a tricky situation. Clutterbuck might well use that as a reason for turning down his application for a warrant. He'd need to explain as diplomatically as possible why he still wanted one and if the conversation went wrong, he'd rather it happened in private. He temporised.

'Some progress, sir, but if you have no objection, I'd rather give you a full report on Monday.'

'Certainly. Not a subject to discuss with the ladies around, eh? But no cause for serious concern, I hope?'

'I trust not, sir.'

Clutterbuck glanced at his wife. 'Good man,' he muttered and turned to her as she and Jane joined them again.

'Your wife and I have been talking about books, Inspector,' she said. 'Are you fond of detective novels too?'

'I like to read, ma'am, but Jane is the expert on them. I prefer the classics.'

'Ah, Miss Austen, Mr Dickens and so forth. Of course one read them all at school.'

'Never been much of a reader myself,' the assistant government agent remarked jovially. '*Wisden* and *The Field* more in my line.'

The Clutterbucks moved on to talk to someone else and Jane giggled. 'Florence Clutterbuck never likes to be outdone.'

'I didn't mean it that way.'

'I know that, but she didn't. Oh look, there's Sergeant Prasanna. We must go and say hello and wish him luck. The poor fellow looks anxious.'

Indeed he did, thought de Silva. Dressed ready to play in his cricket whites, the sergeant looked like nothing so much as a tethered deer that has just sighted a hungry leopard. A moment later a bevy of middle-aged ladies dressed in splendid saris engulfed him.

'Good afternoon, Inspector, sir. Good afternoon, Mrs de Silva.'

De Silva turned to see Constable Nadar, also dressed in cricket whites, with his wife and baby son. Nadar introduced them then gestured in the direction of his colleague. 'Sergeant Prasanna has many aunties,' he said with a grin.

'Perhaps you ought to rescue him,' said de Silva. 'I expect you'll both be needed soon at the pavilion.'

Nadar nodded.

'Do stay and talk to us, my dear,' said Jane to his wife as he hurried away. She stroked the baby's cheek. 'What a dear little boy. He looks very content.'

The girl smiled shyly. 'He cries a little, but not too much.'

'Is your husband looking forward to the match?'

'I think so, ma'am, but he is afraid he will let the side down. He is not so good at cricket as Sergeant Prasanna.'

'Never mind that. The important thing is to take part.'

'I hope so, ma'am.'

They chatted for a few minutes then Mrs Nadar took the baby and went to join her family.

The Clutterbucks had invited the de Silvas to join their party for lunch and it would have been impolite to refuse, although it wasn't the company de Silva would have chosen under the circumstances. Neither did he relish the prospect of another meal of British food. Dubiously, he studied the slices of ham and gelatinous pork pie on his plate. Tied up to his master's chair leg, Darcy the Labrador licked his lips and sniffed the air. De Silva wondered if there was some way that he could convey the contents of his plate to the dog without being noticed. Clearly, Darcy would enjoy them far more than he was going to.

He heard a scraping of chairs and realised that the assistant government agent and the other men at the table were standing to greet someone. Hastily, he jumped up and saw that it was Madeleine Renshaw with Hamish beside her.

'Is your husband here?' Florence Clutterbuck asked when greetings had been exchanged. 'You must both come and join us.' She beckoned to one of the attendants who had served the meal and were now hovering to receive further orders. 'Fetch more chairs.'

'Please don't trouble,' Madeleine Renshaw said – awkwardly, de Silva thought. 'I'm not sure where my husband has got to. Hamish and I were just going to look for him.'

De Silva glanced at Hamish who was crouching on the floor petting Darcy. The dog seemed to be enjoying the attention, rolling onto his back with a happy groan for his stomach to be scratched. 'Fond of dogs, eh, lad?' Archie Clutterbuck asked genially.

Hamish nodded. 'Yes, sir.' He looked at his mother. 'May I stay and play with him?'

'Do let him, Mrs Renshaw,' Florence said kindly. 'Why don't you sit down too?' She fanned herself. 'It's very hot to be rushing around. I'll send one of the servants to look for your husband and tell him where you are.'

'Thank you, but I'd like to walk about for a while. But if Hamish won't be a nuisance, it would be very kind if he could stay.'

'No trouble at all. The cricket will be starting soon, and he can sit with us until you come back. He might like to take Darcy for a little walk before then.'

Hamish beamed.

As he watched Madeleine Renshaw walk away, de Silva wondered why she was so reluctant to be saved a walk in the midday heat.

The servants brought out dishes of wobbly pink blanc-mange decorated with glacé cherries and slivers of angelica. To de Silva's taste buds, the pudding was as bland as the rest of the meal but at least it was sweet.

The lunch party broke up and de Silva and Jane found seats in the front row of the stand and waited for the match to begin.

A polite ripple of applause greeted the players as they came onto the field. 'Who's our captain?' asked de Silva, not recognising the tallish man with a neatly clipped moustache who led out the Nuala team.

'He's the new doctor. His name is Hebden. Apparently, he's a first-class batsman and an Oxford Blue so that should help us. That means he played for Oxford University,' she added.

'I know what it means. You forget that I know many of your strange English expressions. You call ladies "bluestockings" when their stockings are not blue, you say something happens "once in a blue moon", but the moon is never blue, and when my roses flower well, you tell me I have a green thumb.'

Hatton won the toss and elected to bowl first. A surveyor from the Forestry Department and Doctor Hebden went into bat.

Hebden made an impressive beginning, confidently driving the balls that Hatton's best bowler sent down and hitting a four and a six in the first fifteen minutes. A rumble of approval animated the Nuala stand, but on the next ball it turned to a gasp of dismay. A googly took him unawares and he was given out lbw.

'Oh dear,' Jane said with a sigh as the doctor walked to the pavilion, his eyes firmly fixed on the ground. 'How disappointing, and his first match here too.'

'Perhaps he was overconfident.'

Jane tapped his sleeve. 'Hush, dear. Play's beginning again.'

The rest of the Nuala team battled on but runs came slowly and the loss of their hoped-for star showed. The heat of the afternoon intensified, and Jane peered at the sky. 'Not a single cloud. I should have brought my parasol. I think it must be in the car. Shanti, would you be a dear?'

'Of course.'

Stepping down from the stand, he set off in the direction of the car park. The sound of leather on willow and desultory clapping followed him.

He was nearly at the track leading to the car park when he noticed two men lounging outside one of the refreshment tents, smoking and drinking whisky. Deep in conversation, they didn't appear to notice him, but he recognised Charles Renshaw and the driver of the Daimler. Renshaw threw down the butt of his cigarette, ground it out with his heel and lit another one. He smoked with jerky movements, staring at the ground. The Daimler's driver appeared to be doing most of the talking. De Silva decided to move on before they saw him. He felt a twinge of pity for Madeleine Renshaw. She seemed more anxious to find her husband than he was to find her.

In the car park he passed the black Daimler and stopped for a moment to admire it. It was a fine car and almost new. It was a pity a few of the metal spokes on the offside rear wheel were slightly bent. Renshaw's friend must have clipped something.

The parasol was in the Morris as Jane had guessed. He

had got it out and turned to go back to the cricket ground when he saw five of the ponies from the lake ambling out of the trees that fringed the car park. He wouldn't put it past the little ruffians to chew off a few wing mirrors. He walked towards them, clapping his hands, and shouting at them to be off, and they turned and trotted away. It was then that he noticed a tall man disappear into the trees and, hurrying in the other direction, a woman wearing a pale-green dress.

By the time he returned to the cricket pitch, play had stopped for tea and the Nuala side had declared at ninety-six for eight.

'Disappointing performance from that fellow Hebden,' growled Archie Clutterbuck as they walked to the tea tent. 'After all the talk about him being a Blue, seemed very rusty to me. I hope your sergeant will be on good form. It looks like we'll need him to save the day.'

In the refreshment tent, as they waited to help themselves to cups of tea and finger sandwiches, de Silva noticed that Madeleine Renshaw had returned and was talking to Florence Clutterbuck and some of the other planters' wives. He steered Jane over to them and while she joined in the conversation, he checked Madeleine's outfit surreptitiously. Yes, her dress was the right shade of pale green. He was sure she was the woman he had seen among the trees.

Play resumed with two hours to go before sunset. De Silva put work concerns out of his mind and concentrated on the game.

'Hatton are a formidable foe,' he remarked to Jane. 'Prasanna and the others will have to pull out all the stops now.'

The afternoon wore on. Denied the clear margin for victory they had anticipated, some of the Nuala team had lost confidence, but luckily Sergeant Prasanna wasn't among them. Inventive and skilful, he bowled a variety of leg spin, googlies and top spinners that tested the Hatton team and kept them guessing. De Silva found it interesting. Prasanna was usually such a diffident young man, but when you put a cricket ball in his hand, he blossomed.

As the shadows lengthened the occupants of both stands fell quiet. 'Ninety-two runs against us,' Jane whispered. 'We might just make it. The light's going fast.'

De Silva took his eyes off the pitch. Swallows were swooping through the air after insects. High above him a flock of egrets flew in perfect arrow-head formation towards the setting sun. It was a time of day he loved.

An exclamation from Jane and a sharp tug on his sleeve snapped his attention back to the match. 'Shanti! Why aren't you watching? Your sergeant is about to become a hero.'

A moment later the Hatton team was all out for ninety-four. The Nuala stand erupted, even Florence Clutterbuck was on her feet. 'Magnificent!' her husband boomed, slapping de Silva on the back. 'Never have done it without your sergeant. Remarkable player!'

De Silva glanced over to where Prasanna was being mobbed by excited admirers who had rushed onto the field. The Hatton team and the rest of the Nuala players were shaking hands and chatting. As players drifted away towards the pavilion or to greet friends and family, Doctor Hebden detached himself from one of the groups and came over to where de Silva and the assistant government agent stood.

'Ah, Hebden!' Clutterbuck shook his hand. 'Not your day, eh?'

Hebden smiled ruefully. 'I'm afraid not, sir. All the credit goes to Sergeant Prasanna.'

He held out his hand. 'I'm David Hebden, and I believe you're Inspector de Silva. You must be proud of your sergeant.'

De Silva shook it. 'Shanti de Silva, and yes, I am very

proud. I knew Prasanna had talent but not quite the extent of it.'

'Well,' said Clutterbuck, still beaming, 'if you gentlemen will excuse me, my wife and I have an engagement this evening and I mustn't keep her waiting. Please tell Prasanna I'm sorry not to congratulate him in person.'

They watched him stride away to where his wife waited. Madeleine Renshaw and her son were once more with her.

Hebden frowned. 'Charles Renshaw's wife left on her own again. I wonder where Renshaw's got to. He's a strange fellow. With such a charming wife, most husbands would be more attentive.'

'I've only a slight acquaintance with Renshaw, but he doesn't seem a ladies' man to me.'

'Quite. Have you met Mrs Renshaw?'

'Only briefly. My wife knows her better.'

'I've come across her several times in my professional capacity. That boy of hers is a source of anxiety.' With a grin, he gestured to where Hamish was playing with Darcy. 'Although to see him running around with the Clutterbucks' dog, you wouldn't think there was much wrong with him. I'm afraid some mothers do tend to translate their own unhappiness into worries about their children.'

He was silent for a moment, his eyes on Madeleine Renshaw as if he had forgotten de Silva was there, then he collected himself. 'Forgive me. I find people's minds an interesting study. But as you are a policeman, I imagine that's something we have in common.'

'Indeed it is.'

'Now, if you'll excuse me, I must go and talk to the Hatton captain before he leaves. It's been a pleasure to meet you. I hope all our meetings will be purely social.'

'Likewise.'

'Doctor Hebden seems a charming man,' Jane remarked as they returned to the Morris. 'Poor Madeleine Renshaw,

I don't think she enjoyed the day much. That husband of hers is as boorish as you said. He turned up with his friend just as the Clutterbucks were offering their official car and chauffeur to take her home and he barely thanked them for looking after his wife.'

They joined the queue of cars leaving the car park. Several vehicles ahead of them, de Silva spotted the black Daimler weaving from left to right as if trying to overtake the slowly moving line. After a few minutes, a series of parps from the Daimler's horn made heads turn then the car veered off the track onto the grass and was soon out of sight.

'What bad manners.' Jane sniffed. 'I expect that man driving's had too much to drink.'

De Silva thought of what he'd seen outside the refreshment tent but decided not to mention it, or his sighting of the woman he was sure was Madeleine Renshaw.

'Probably.'

They reached the road and by the time they arrived home, darkness had fallen. He looked up at the sky. Rags of cloud had moved in, hiding some of the stars. Lucky it had been dry for the match. The weather might not be so good tomorrow.

CHAPTER 9

It rained in the middle of the night. Great waves of water that lashed the roof and smacked against the windows. Listening to the downpour, he groaned at the thought of how it would be ruining his roses, but in the morning the damage was less than he had feared.

Mist filled the valley and a few trails of it drifted across the bungalow's lawn. A feeling of well-being filled him as he inhaled the smell of damp vegetation mingled with flower scents intensified by the warm rain.

In the dining room breakfast waited. He rubbed his hands at the sight of tureens of string hoppers, hot rice, and curries.

'You look cheerful, dear,' remarked Jane. 'Did the roses survive better than you expected?'

He ladled curry onto a mound of string hoppers. 'I was pleasantly surprised.'

'Do you have plans for the day?'

'Nothing in particular.'

The telephone rang in the hall and de Silva heard one of the servants answer it. He frowned. Calls on a Sunday morning were unusual, especially so early. The servant came to the dining room door. 'It's for you, sahib. Doctor Hebden wishes to speak with you.'

De Silva wiped his lips with his napkin and went to the phone. 'Good morning, Doctor Hebden. What can I do for you?'

'I'm sorry to call so early, Inspector. Can you get up to the Renshaws' place straight away? I'd be grateful if your wife would come with you.'

'Of course, but why do you need us?'

'It's Charles Renshaw. He's been found dead.'

* * *

Hebden's car was parked in the yard at the Five Palms plantation, but otherwise the place seemed deserted. Where workers had sorted leaves outside the factory on de Silva's previous visit, there was only tea dust and a few empty wicker baskets. The silence had an eerie quality.

The door to the factory building was open, so they went in and followed the murmur of voices to the first floor. Doctor Hebden stood at the far end of the withering room beside one of the long tanks. He looked up and raised a hand in greeting. De Silva went over to him and looked down into the tank. Renshaw lay among the drying leaves. His barrel chest was bare but a loose pair of cotton trousers with a drawstring waist covered the lower part of his body. Only the waxy pallor of his face and the tinge of grey around his lips betrayed that he was dead. The random thought drifted into de Silva's mind that he wasn't going to need that warrant now.

Jane let out a gasp and gripped the side of the tank. Hebden put a hand on her shoulder. 'I'm sorry to expose you to such a shock, Mrs de Silva. Would you like to sit down somewhere? I'll send for a glass of water for you.'

She shook her head mutely.

'Who found him?' asked de Silva.

'The night watchman. He says Renshaw came back late yesterday with his friend in the black Daimler. They carried on drinking in Renshaw's office. The friend – the night watchman says his name is David Leung – called him up to the first floor at about midnight. He told him his master wasn't feeling too well and would sleep on the camp bed in his office. He wasn't to be disturbed, so the watchman should make his last round of the factory right away. Leung waited while he did so then they left together. The watchman locked up and went back to his quarters.

'The next morning around dawn, he was on his early round when he heard the noise of something battering against one of the windows. He unlocked the main doors, went in, and found a big fruit bat. He had no idea how it got there. He was sure all the doors and windows were closed when he left the previous night. He tried to shoo the bat out – those damn things leave droppings everywhere – but it flew up to the first floor. He chased it into the withering room where he found Renshaw's body.'

'Who else knows he's dead?'

'Renshaw's manager. The watchman went to him rather than going down to the bungalow. He called me and I came straight up. I haven't spoken with Archie Clutterbuck yet. I'm afraid that once his wife knows, it'll be all round town. Can't be helped of course, but I thought we ought to break the news to Madeleine Renshaw first. That's why I asked you to come, Mrs de Silva. It will help to have another woman here.'

'I'll do my best, but it's bound to be a terrible shock for the poor lady.'

De Silva leant over the tank. A strong smell of whisky rose from Renshaw's body.

'What's your view on the cause of death?'

'There's no sign of external injury apart from some minor bruising and abrasion to the face and body. He might have stumbled on the way between the Daimler and the factory building or inside it. These concrete floors are rough enough to do that level of damage. The watchman found him half

73

hidden under the leaves in the tank, so there's a possibility he asphyxiated while under the influence of alcohol, but it seems remote. If he was drunk enough not to notice that he'd fallen into the tank, I don't see how he would have been agile enough to have hoisted himself up those.' He pointed to the set of wooden steps close by.

'I think it's more likely that he was half sober and had some idea about testing the moisture content of the leaves. The exertion brought on a seizure, and he collapsed into the tank. He's not consulted me since I've been here, but I glanced at my predecessor's notes on him before I came up. About six months ago, Doctor MacCallum diagnosed a heart problem. It's not conclusive evidence but the grey tinge around the mouth and at the ends of the fingertips are usually reliable indications of a heart attack. Also the way the body is contorted, particularly the clenching of the right hand. In heart seizures, the first symptom would normally be excruciating pain in one or both of the arms.'

'What about the time of death?'

'I arrived here at ten past eight and took the body's temperature shortly after that. My estimate is that Renshaw hadn't been dead for more than a few hours, so five o'clock or thereabouts.'

'Hmm. Thank you, doctor.'

Hebden looked at his watch. 'If you're in agreement, I'll use the telephone here to make arrangements to have the body removed to the morgue. After that I think we should inform Madeleine Renshaw.'

De Silva nodded.

* * *

Bee-eaters darted among the trees in the plantation bungalow's garden; the raucous cry of a peacock splintered the quiet. The sound of the doorbell died away before they heard shuffling inside and the grating of bolts being drawn back. A drowsy-eyed servant peered at them.

'Tell your mistress that Inspector de Silva and Doctor Hebden are here to see her,' said Hebden.

'What is it, Asha?' Madeleine Renshaw appeared in the hallway. Not dressed for visitors in a plain, grey dress with a Kashmiri shawl thrown around her shoulders, she looked tired. At the sight of de Silva and Hebden, her eyes widened.

Hebden went to her and took her hands. 'We need to talk in private, ma'am.'

She dismissed the servant. 'Has something happened to Charles?' she asked when the man was out of earshot. 'He was drinking far too much yesterday, but it's a waste of time telling him. Has he had an accident? Please, tell me quickly.'

She noticed Jane and turned pale. A tremor came into her voice. 'It's serious, isn't it?'

'Come and sit down.'

Hebden led her into the drawing room and the de Silvas followed. She sank into a chair. 'Has he been taken to hospital?'

Jane and de Silva looked at each other. There was never an easy way of breaking bad news to the family of the deceased.

'I'm afraid I'm the bearer of very bad tidings,' Hebden said quietly.

Madeleine Renshaw seemed to curl in on herself. Like a caterpillar alarmed by the touch of a human hand, thought de Silva. 'Charles is dead, isn't he?' she whispered. 'That's what you've come to tell me.'

Jane put an arm around the young woman's rigid shoulders. 'I'm so sorry.'

A low, keening sound swelled, and Madeleine started to rock back and forward. Hebden went to the door and shouted for a servant. 'Bring some brandy,' he barked at the startled man.

When it came, he raised her head and held the glass to her lips. 'Drink it slowly. Small sips, that's it.'

She wiped the tears from her cheeks and swallowed a little brandy then went into a paroxysm of coughing and pushed the glass away.

'Hamish is with his ayah in the garden. I don't want him to know yet,' she gasped. 'I need to think of what to say.'

Hebden nodded. 'It might be best if you go and lie down. The servants can tell him you're resting for the morning.'

'If you'd like me to stay, I will,' said Jane.

'Thank you.'

'Did you know your husband had a weak heart, ma'am?' asked Hebden.

'I knew he took pills for it. Doctor MacCallum gave them to him, but he said they wouldn't be enough on their own. The best remedy was for Charles to stop drinking.' Her voice dwindled. 'But he wouldn't, and now—'

She buried her face in her hands once more.

Jane helped her to her feet. 'Let's go to your room so you can lie down, my dear. Shanti, would you ask one of the servants to bring us some tea? It might be preferable to brandy.'

De Silva found a servant and, ignoring the man's inquisitive expression, ordered him to take tea to his mistress's room.

'I may as well go back up to the factory,' said Hebden. 'Mrs Renshaw is in good hands and the undertakers said they'd come quickly.'

'They may have to wait awhile. I'd like to examine the body before they take it away.'

Hebden frowned. 'I've had a pretty thorough look, but if you want to.'

'I do, but I didn't think it was appropriate with my wife present.'

As they left the bungalow's drive, the undertakers' black station wagon came into sight, negotiating the rutted road to the factory at a crawl. De Silva went on ahead leaving Hebden to speak to them. He easily outpaced the party and was in the withering room by the time the men arrived. Three of them lifted Renshaw's body from its musty bed and de Silva knelt on the floor beside it and began a careful examination. He was aware that Hebden never took his eyes off what he was doing.

At last he stood up. 'You're right, Doctor Hebden. The only signs of damage to the body are the abrasions and bruises you mentioned. No cuts or bullet wounds. He didn't vomit and evacuation of the bowels is insignificant.'

Hebden grunted. 'I'm glad we're in agreement,' he said with a tinge of sarcasm. 'If you have no objection, I suggest we let these fellows take the body away now.'

'Certainly. I'll stay here a moment. I'd like to be sure there's nothing suspicious in the vicinity of where the body lay.'

Another grunt from Hebden suggested to de Silva that the doctor didn't like his opinion being questioned. Still, that couldn't be helped.

The undertakers' men moved Renshaw's body to a stretcher and, with Hebden accompanying them, started down the stairs.

'Ah, here you are,' he said when he returned a few minutes later to find de Silva in the office, examining the camp bed. 'Anything of interest?'

'No, nothing in the withering tank but leaves, and here,' he indicated the camp bed, 'the sheets are very crumpled but that's not surprising with a hot night and a drunken man.' He pointed to an empty whisky bottle and two glasses on the desk.

Hebden picked up a nearby bottle of pills and examined the label. 'Probably the ones MacCallum prescribed that

Mrs Renshaw mentioned. I'll take them with me. Don't want them falling into the wrong hands.'

One by one, de Silva opened the doors of the cupboards on the wall above the filing cabinets. Some contained boxes of paper, typewriter ribbons, string, rubber bands and paper clips; others held a few mismatched glasses and more whisky bottles. When he opened the door of the last one, he smelled spices and dried herbs. He pulled out a bag of what looked like tea and sniffed it. The first scent he inhaled was rose, followed by cardamom, ginger, and liquorice.

'What's that?' asked Hebden.

'My guess is that it's pitta tea. An Ayurvedic remedy for poor digestion. It's also supposed to cool the body and reduce inflammation of the skin. I remember Renshaw had a nasty rash when I saw him here.'

Hebden frowned. 'That's strange. I know that occasionally my patients consult Ayurvedic doctors too and I have no objection, but I wouldn't have thought Renshaw was one of them.'

'Neither would I, but then people often surprise me.'

'Ah well, it's of no significance now and there's nothing more I can do here. I'll stop at the bungalow on my way back to Nuala. I've got something in my bag that will help Mrs Renshaw to sleep if she needs it. I'll come back later today and see how she's getting on. Is your wife prepared to stay with her for a while?'

'I'm sure she will if it would be a help.'

'Good. No doubt we'll be in touch soon.'

His footsteps rang on the metal stairs, and he was gone. De Silva had the clear impression that there was no doubt in the doctor's mind as to the cause of Renshaw's death. His concern now was for the planter's widow.

The bag of dried leaves was still in de Silva's hand. He took another pinch and sniffed it. Yes, almost certainly it was pitta tea. He looked around the room and noticed a china cup in the cracked enamel sink under the window. It had obviously been used and not washed up as a small amount of brown liquid was still in the bottom of the cup. He swirled it around and caught the scent of roses, liquorice, and spices as before, but there was a faint tang of something else that even his good sense of smell was unable to identify. He put the cup back in the sink then changed his mind. He would take it with him and the dried tea too. Downstairs, he carefully stowed both in a box in the Morris's trunk.

After a few words with Renshaw's manager, he started up the engine and set off down the rutted road. It was only as he passed the bungalow that it struck him that Madeleine Renshaw hadn't asked how her husband had died.

CHAPTER 10

The ceiling of the Crown's vast lobby glowed with panels of stained glass set in a tracery of polished wood that suggested the leaves and branches of a great tree. It was a place of glamour and dreams, thought de Silva as he walked through the magnificent oak and glass doors. Ever since he and Jane had seen the film *Grand Hotel* on one of their regular trips to Nuala's cinema, the Crown reminded him of it. He almost expected to see Greta Garbo, swathed in velvet and fur, sashaying across the foyer with that faraway look in her eyes. He hid a smile as Sergeant Prasanna gasped and hung back before following across the gleaming marble floor as if it might swallow him up at any moment.

If the receptionist was surprised to receive a visit from the police that Monday morning, he was too well trained to show it.

'I've arranged to meet Mr David Leung. Please tell him I'm here.'

'Certainly, Inspector. I'll telephone his room.'

De Silva watched him make the call and replace the receiver. 'Mr Leung will be with you shortly. He suggests you meet in the library. Would you like someone to show you the way?'

'There's no need, thank you.'

People come and go, nothing ever happens, thought de Silva, recalling the opening lines of *Grand Hotel* as he and Prasanna walked to the library down a corridor wide enough for two bullock carts to pass each other. But subsequently, as anyone who had watched the film knew, a great deal had happened. A lesson that you should always expect the unexpected. Or was he the only one who believed that?

After Renshaw's death, Archie Clutterbuck had seemed all too eager to accept Doctor Hebden's view that the cause of death was heart failure. 'Hebden's a sound man,' he'd said, a note of exasperation creeping into his voice. 'I've told him I'm happy to rely on his judgement and I think you should be too, de Silva. Where will going around asking a lot of questions get us? Renshaw was just the sort of fellow who's likely to have the old ticker give up on him. Believe me, I've seen plenty of his kind. In any event, in this climate, it's best to get on with burying him. Better for the widow too. I'm sure Madeleine Renshaw will be relieved to get the funeral over.'

The library's plum velvet curtains framed tall windows that nevertheless let in very little light. Dark leather sofas and low tables furnished it, and the walls were lined with yard after yard of books with gold-tooled spines. The room smelled of tobacco and beeswax polish. Brass reading lamps with bottle green shades stood on the tables. De Silva pulled the chain on one of them and a pool of light descended. He sat down and pointed to an upright chair by one of the windows. 'When Leung comes, you'd better sit there to write notes.'

'Yes, sir.'

'And, Prasanna, try not to look like a rabbit in the headlights.'

'Sorry, sir.'

The door swung open, and David Leung strode in. He wore a dark suit, and the cuffs of his white shirt were fastened with chunky gold links. His gold watch was obviously expensive. 'Inspector de Silva? I'm David Leung. I understand you wanted to see me.'

De Silva nodded. 'Good morning, Mr Leung. Thank you for being so prompt. I just have a few routine questions. If you've no objection, my sergeant here will take notes.'

'Do I have an option, Inspector? I assume this is about my late friend Charles Renshaw. A tragic occurrence. I understand from what people are saying here that it was his heart. I was very shocked when I heard the news. As you probably know, I was with him that evening. When I left the plantation to return to Nuala, I had no idea he was in any danger.' He shook his head. 'I blame myself for not being more perceptive. But I forget my manners, Inspector. May I offer you a drink?'

'No, thank you.'

'I hope you don't mind if I do.'

Leung went to a sideboard on which stood several decanters and some cut-glass tumblers. He poured a whisky then returned to his chair. Swirling the whisky in his glass, he leant back. 'Please, ask away, Inspector. I'll do anything I can to help. Charles Renshaw was a dear friend.'

'I understand you were with Mr Renshaw most of the day at the cricket match. Is that correct?'

Leung nodded.

'Some observers have mentioned that your conversation seemed heated at times.'

Leung frowned. 'What observers?'

'I'm not at liberty to tell you that, sir.'

Leung shrugged. 'Very well. It may have looked that way, I suppose. Poor Charles had business troubles that I was trying to help him with. He wasn't a man who found it easy to take advice, even from a friend. I had hoped, however, that we were making progress.'

'Was Mrs Renshaw aware of her husband's difficulties?'

'Madeleine? Good Lord no. Charles didn't want her upset.'

'But you drove them both home after the cricket.'

'Yes, but Charles insisted she remain in the dark. When we reached Five Palms, he muttered to me that he wanted to talk more. As it turned out, he also wanted to drink more. I tried to dissuade him, but I fear whisky was Charles's way of dealing with his troubles.'

The scratch of Prasanna's pen filled the brief silence.

'So, you dropped Mrs Renshaw and her son off at the bungalow and went up to the factory.'

'Yes.'

'If Mr Renshaw wanted to talk, wouldn't it have been more comfortable at the bungalow?'

'Probably, but Charles wanted to go to his office. He had some papers he wished me to see. He was rather paranoid about being overheard too. I'm afraid he could be very mistrustful of Madeleine, and he often accused their servants of listening at doors.'

'Did he have any justification for that?'

'None to my knowledge.'

'You say that Mr Renshaw carried on drinking. Could you estimate how much he'd had by the time you left him?'

Leung thought for a moment. 'I believe he had three, maybe four, whiskies, but adding those to what he drank over the course of the day, I'd say half a bottle.'

'Was that a normal amount for him?'

'Not unusual, I'm afraid. For as long as I can remember, Charles was a heavy drinker. It didn't stop him functioning and he probably drank a bit less when he was busy at the factory, but it was getting worse.'

De Silva's eyebrows rose. No wonder the plantation was in trouble.

'And for how long had you known him?'

'About five years. We met in Colombo. We were both involved in a variety of the same businesses. That was before Charles inherited the plantation.'

'Was Mr Renshaw successful then?'

'Moderately, but I'm afraid he often rubbed people up the wrong way. Not a good idea in business.'

'But you got on with him.'

'Perhaps I have a thicker skin than most. Charles was a good man under the gruff exterior.'

'According to the night watchman, you left the factory at about midnight.'

'That's correct. I came back to the hotel and went to bed. It had been a long day. I slept late that morning, breakfasted in my room and worked on some papers. It wasn't until I went down to lunch that I heard the news. Later I received your message.'

'Apart from the night watchman, did you notice anyone else up at the factory?'

'No, the place was deserted. When I passed the bunga-low, all the lights were out too. Presumably, Madeleine had retired to bed.'

'Were you aware that Mr Renshaw was taking medicine for his heart?'

'He mentioned his doctor had prescribed something for a heart murmur, that was all. He told me it was a fuss about nothing. He rarely took the pills and was tempted to throw them away.'

'Did he ever talk to you about Ayurvedic medicine?'

Leung's expression was impassive. 'Charles was a man who dismissed what he referred to as "quackery" even more roundly than conventional medicine. He regarded illness as a symptom of weakness.'

He swirled his whisky glass again and drained it. 'Sadly, that view seems to have been his undoing. I feel extremely sorry for Madeleine. How has she taken the news?'

'Very distressed, as you would expect.'

He nodded. 'I plan to stay on for the funeral, of course. I hope to have the opportunity of talking to her and offering my condolences then.'

'Do you live in Colombo?'

'Part of the time when the needs of my business require me to.'

'And may I ask what your line of business is?'

'Commodities. Import export.'

He looked at his watch. 'Forgive me, Inspector, but if there's nothing else that I can help you with, I have a lunch appointment at the Empire Club.'

'Nothing for the moment, Mr Leung.' De Silva stood up. 'Thank you for your time.'

They left the hotel and he turned out of the drive in the direction of the station. After a short distance he pulled into a side road and switched off the engine.

'Is something wrong, sir?' asked Prasanna.

'I want to go back and check what time Leung returned to the hotel on Sunday morning, but I'd rather do it when I know he's gone.'

'Do you think he was lying about when he left the factory?'

De Silva shook his head. 'Probably not. The night watchman corroborated his story, but it's always worth checking everything. Being a policeman for as long as I have has taught me that. If Leung left the factory at around midnight, even allowing for driving in the dark and the state of the roads – if you remember, it rained very heavily overnight – he should have been back at the hotel not much later than one o'clock.'

The sound of a powerful engine swelled and with a roar, the Daimler swept past the end of the road. When he had waited for the sound to die away, de Silva drove back to the hotel. 'Go in and see if you can find out who was on duty that night and if they remember what time Leung returned.'

'What do I say if someone asks why I want to know, sir?'

'Tell them it's a routine inquiry. Oh, and say it's confidential.'

De Silva tapped the steering wheel, humming under his breath as he waited for Prasanna to return. He admired the roses in the flowerbeds that flanked the hotel drive. A magnificent wisteria, heavy with purple flowers, smothered the walls on either side of the porch. The building's style, with black beams set into white walls, was so English.

'I spoke to the manager, sir. The night porter is off duty sleeping, but he'll ask him when he comes on again. I said I'd come back.'

'You'll have to learn not to let these people fob you off, Prasanna.'

'I'm sorry, sir.' Prasanna looked chastened. 'I'll go back and tell him to wake the man up, shall I?'

De Silva started the engine. 'No, you can leave it this time. It's just a detail and it will keep. This afternoon we'll go up to the plantation. I'd like another look around.'

* * *

They drove into the yard at the plantation and de Silva turned off the Morris's engine. The only sound was the twittering of birds and there was no sign of workers on the tea terraces. It was disturbing how quickly things fell apart, thought de Silva as he waited for Prasanna to return with a key.

'Where is everyone?' he asked when the sergeant reappeared.

'Most of them have stayed down at the labour lines, sir. The manager says he's having trouble persuading them to come back to work. They're afraid it's unlucky to come up after their master died here.'

'I expect it's the last thing on Madeleine Renshaw's mind, but she'll have to find a way of dealing with that or the business will be in even worse shape.' He took the large iron key from Prasanna. 'Right, we'd best get on with this.'

As the metal door swung open, releasing the trapped heat, de Silva stepped back. 'Phew! You may take your jacket off if you want, Prasanna.'

Prasanna didn't wait to be told again.

Dim light filtered from the high window on the first-floor landing. The scent of tea permeated the air. 'I'm going to take another look in Renshaw's office,' said de Silva. 'I want you to walk around everywhere else. If you see anything you think odd – anything at all – come and tell me.'

'Very well, sir.'

The heat in Renshaw's office was even more intense than it had been downstairs. De Silva loosened his tie and went to the window. After a battle with the latch and a firm nudge from his elbow it opened, letting in a modicum of cooler air.

He moved along the filing cabinets, opening each one. There seemed to be nothing unusual about their contents. Turning his attention to the desk, he found a few photographs. A couple of them showed Renshaw with Madeleine at the bungalow, squinting into the sun and smiling. The rest looked to be from an earlier time. A vigorous-looking man with a bushy beard featured in many of them, either standing with groups of workers or supervising the loading and unloading of carts. De Silva guessed he was the man Renshaw had taken the plantation over from. If that was correct, it seemed to have been a more prosperous place in his day.

The desk's last drawer opened halfway then stuck. He peered in and saw it contained cardboard wallets, one of which was jamming the drawer. With his hand slid as far as it would go, he pressed down on the pile and pulled too sharply. The drawer clattered to the floor.

He picked it up, put it on the desk and lifted out the contents. A crumpled sheet of thick paper at the bottom had been the cause of the problem. He laid it to one side and examined the wallets. Most of them were empty, but a few contained old statements from Renshaw's bank. When he was satisfied that there was nothing unusual about the entries, de Silva put the wallets back in the drawer and turned his attention to the crumpled paper. He raised an eyebrow. It was a letter headed with the name of a loan company he didn't recognise – Asian Ventures. The size of the scheduled loan repayments bore out that Renshaw was in financial difficulties. He folded the letter and put it in his pocket. There was an old friend and colleague in Colombo who might be able to throw some light on the identity of the company. He would contact him.

He looked at the time on the clock on the wall. Surely, he and Prasanna couldn't have been at the factory that long? He checked his watch. No, only a little over half an hour had passed. Renshaw should have had that clock fixed. Time to find out if Prasanna had uncovered anything of interest.

'I'm down here, sir.' De Silva followed the sound of Prasanna's voice to a cluttered storeroom at the back of the ground floor. The sergeant held up a black carcass by one bony wing. 'A fruit bat, sir.'

De Silva's nose wrinkled. 'I can see that, Sergeant.'

'It's probably the bat the night watchman saw. It must have been trying to get out.' He indicated a small window with a rusty metal frame in the wall opposite the door. The floor beneath it was thick with droppings.

'It didn't have much luck. It doesn't look as if that window gets opened very often.'

'I thought that at first, sir, but see—' Prasanna ran his hand over the glass and then held it up to show the dust and strands of cobwebs. 'Yet where the window meets the frame, it's cleaner.'

De Silva studied the frame and toggled the latch. 'This is very loose and there's enough of a gap between the frame and the window to slip in something thin and lift it. Open it, Prasanna, and see if the hole's big enough for you to climb out.'

A pile of wooden boxes stood against the wall near the window. Prasanna pulled one over and climbed onto it, then he opened the window and swung his legs through the aperture. He twisted to let his hips and shoulders follow. A few moments later he was on the other side.

'Hmm,' said de Silva. 'It's possible someone managed to lift the latch from outside and gain entrance this way after Leung left. They closed the window on their way out but by that time, the bat had flown in. Instinct led it to try and get out by the same route, but it was too late. Well done, Prasanna, you can come back inside now.'

Prasanna pulled himself up and clambered through the window. 'Why do you think someone would have wanted to get in, sir?' he asked, brushing the dust from his trousers with his hands. 'Burglary?'

'Not burglary, Sergeant: murder.'

Prasanna stopped brushing. 'So you do think the circumstances are suspicious, sir.'

'Yes. Despite what Doctor Hebden says, I'm not convinced Renshaw died of a heart attack.'

'But who would want him dead?'

Briefly, de Silva explained about Hari Gooptu.

'Do you think it might be a revenge attack?'

'I'm not sure about anything yet, but we can't rule it out. The timing's very close and that makes me suspicious. The signs on Renshaw's body might indicate suffocation rather than a heart attack. There was no serious bruising but if he was in a drunken stupor, a murderer wouldn't have needed much force to subdue him. There were the grazes, but they might have been caused by a fall. They could, however, also be evidence that someone dragged his body from his office to the withering tank.'

'Could it be that Gooptu came back?'

'Maybe. It's not clear to me yet how badly he's injured, or even if he's still alive. If not him, it might be one or several of the other workers wanting revenge on his behalf.'

Prasanna's expression had grown more solemn by the minute.

De Silva chuckled. 'We may have more excitement than we expected, eh? I think it's time we paid a visit to the labour lines.'

* * *

A dusty track led from the factory yard to the area where the tea workers lived in squat huts built of mud brick and roofed with dried palm leaves. Children wearing nothing but dirty loincloths stopped their games to stare at the interlopers. A few women sat outside their huts making pieces of rough cloth on rudimentary looms. Their menfolk, huddled in small groups on the red ground, watched with anger or wariness in their eyes. Even if it wasn't because they had a murderer in their midst, it was understandable, thought de Silva. Their lives were hard but at least when Renshaw was alive, they had shelter and some wages. His death threw their futures into doubt.

'It's going to be hard to get any of them to talk, sir,' muttered Prasanna.

Out of the corner of his eye, de Silva noticed that one of the older boys held a flat piece of wood. There was a ball at his feet. 'See if you can persuade the children to play cricket with you, Sergeant.'

Prasanna walked over to the boy and pointed to the ball. Hesitantly, the boy handed it to him. The sergeant took a few strides backwards and prepared to bowl, indicating to the boy that he should be ready. His face relaxed in a grin as the improvised cricket bat made contact and the ball flew up and away raising a little cloud of dust where it landed. Another boy ran to fetch it back then one by one, more joined in the game. Some of the women stopped weaving and watched with toothless smiles. One of the men started to laugh, and soon the atmosphere had lightened.

De Silva studied the men. He picked one who only glanced at the game and spent more time covertly studying him. Probably, he was the most likely to give him the information he sought in exchange for a few annas.

He beckoned the man over and asked a few questions, eliciting the information that he had noticed no one missing from the labour lines on the night Renshaw died. It was true that Gooptu had been flogged before his dismissal, but the man hadn't witnessed it and wasn't sure how serious his injuries were. He did, however, know that Gooptu had gone to his village in the jungle.

De Silva produced some more coins. 'Can you take us to it?'

The man nodded and took the money. 'When do you want to go? It is far to walk. About a day from here.'

'In which direction?'

'Down into the lowland. There is a road until the last hour maybe.'

'We'll come for you just after dawn. Be at the factory yard.'

The man waggled his head.

'What's your name?'

'Akash.'

'Thank you, Akash. There'll be more money for you when you bring us back safely.'

The cricket game had reached fever pitch, the children jumping up and down with excitement and shouting encouragement while the adults watched smiling. Prasanna was in to bat now. It seemed a pity to tear him away, but the light would be going soon anyway.

When de Silva called him over, he held out the ball. 'It's a cheap one from the market. Not much life left in it, especially after today. I've got a better one at home I can bring them.'

'We'll be back in the morning.'

The Morris jolted down the rutted track towards the public road. As they passed the gate to the bungalow, he wondered whether to stop to see Jane as she was still with Madeleine, but it might be hard to explain his reasons for being at the plantation. He would telephone her later on.

Approaching Nuala on the road that ran along the side of the lake, he had to stop suddenly as he came out of a bend, narrowly avoiding a group of ponies that stood there drowsing in the evening sun. He honked the Morris's horn, but none of them moved.

'You'd better get out, Prasanna.'

The sergeant opened the door and clapped his hands, but it took a few minutes before the ponies wandered back to the grass. As one ambled past the Morris, de Silva saw how the damp streaks on its cheeks were encrusted with black flies. The poor creatures should have fields to live in, not the dusty roads.

Prasanna got back into the Morris. 'When this business with Renshaw's over,' said de Silva, 'we'd better step up our efforts to find the owners. Otherwise sooner or later there'll be an accident.'

* * *

Later he telephoned Jane from home.

'How are you getting on? How's Mrs Renshaw?'

'Oh, I'm alright. Madeleine's been resting in her room most of the afternoon, so I've played with Hamish. He's a dear little chap. He's been telling me about what he learns with his tutors. He's obviously a bright little boy. That wretched bird of his though, it's a terrible nuisance.'

'Why?'

'I can't imagine where it's learnt so much foul language. It curses like a stevedore.'

He chuckled. 'Perhaps you should send for Florence Clutterbuck to lecture it on the error of its ways.'

'That would be even worse. Seriously, poor Madeleine is so upset by the bird. If it wasn't for the fact Hamish is so fond of it, I think it would have gone long ago.'

'Has she said much about her husband?'

'Not really. It's hard to tell how she feels. It's as if everything's dammed up inside her.' She sighed. 'Twice a widow and she's still very young. And with the responsibility of the plantation on her shoulders now.'

De Silva didn't like to mention the letter he'd seen from the loan company. If they foreclosed, the plantation wouldn't be Madeleine's concern for long.

'When are you coming home?' he asked instead.

'I'd like to stay a few more days, at least until after the funeral. Maybe she'll find it easier to talk once it's over and there'll be something I can do to help.'

'Whatever you think is best.'

'Thank you, dear. I'm sorry to leave you on your own.'

'Oh, I'll be fine. Although I miss you, of course,' he added hastily.

'I should hope so. Now, it's time Hamish went to bed, I'd better go. Will you call me again tomorrow?'

'I promise. Goodnight, my love.'

'Goodnight, dear.'

CHAPTER 11

De Silva did up the top button of his overcoat and wrapped his muffler around his neck. He was glad that the leather driving gloves he wore had a woollen lining.

Sergeant Prasanna shivered in the passenger seat with the travelling rug Jane always insisted on carrying in the Morris draped around him like a shawl. De Silva grinned. 'I hope we don't run across any of your girlfriends. It's not a flattering look.'

'Perhaps it would be a good thing, sir,' the sergeant said glumly.

'Your mother still trying to marry you off, eh?'

'Yes, sir.'

The grey dawn light revealed the plantation worker Akash waiting for them in the factory yard. Clad in an old sarong, with a length of homespun cloth around his shoulders, he looked even colder than Prasanna. He climbed gingerly onto the dickey seat and clung to the bar dividing it from the front as they drove off.

By the time they reached the place where Akash indicated that the road ended, the sun was up, and the air was already warm. De Silva found a place to park, took off his coat and muffler and sent Prasanna to find someone to watch the car while they were away. 'Tell them I'll pay them well when we come back.'

The rice fields on either side soon gave way to jungle.

The path became steep, then levelled and narrowed to meander along the side of a hill.

A network of tree roots protruded from the parched earth and de Silva had to watch his step to make sure he didn't trip. He prayed to any god who would like to listen that no snakes lay in wait.

Below them an occasional glint of silver showed that a small stream ran through the ravine beneath a tangle of fallen trees and creepers. The air clung to de Silva's body, heavy with moisture. He started to sweat, and the powerful smell of rotting vegetation made his stomach queasy. It was a long time since he had walked in the jungle, and he had forgotten how tiring it was if you were not used to it. He slowed his pace to conserve his energy, letting Prasanna and Akash walk ahead.

Despite the discomfort, he reflected, there was beauty in the jungle. Yet there was struggle too. It presented a kind of metaphor for human life; the big bully-boy trees thrusting up toward the sky, while the smaller, weaker ones lived in the understorey. Then there were the passengers: mosses in a dozen shades of green or grey, ferns, lianas, and orchids with pale, gnarled roots like dead men's fingers. All of them depended for their lifeblood on other plants or their decomposing remains.

Just as he thought he would have to rest – surely the walk was taking far longer than the hour Akash had said – they emerged into a clearing where a man with a knife was shaving curls of bark from a slender tree. The delightful smell of cinnamon revived de Silva's spirits.

The man clearly recognised Akash and left his work to take them to the village. A pack of skinny dogs barked as they drew close. Their new guide picked up a stick and threw it at the leader who yelped and backed away. 'Bad,' he grunted.

They reached a scattering of mud huts, each with a porch made of palm fronds propped up by thin tree trunks.

Children played in the dirt, but they looked a little better fed than the ones at the labour lines. There were some goats and two tethered cows as well as a flock of scarlet-wattled jungle fowl strutting between the huts. Sacks of maize and rice were stacked under many of the porches. These people were farmers. In a good year, their diet would be reasonable.

De Silva beckoned to Akash. 'Where's Gooptu?'

'You wait. I speak to his wife. Gooptu very sick. Might be sleeping.' De Silva frowned as Akash disappeared into one of the huts with the cinnamon cutter. He would be angry if they had come all this way for nothing.

But a few moments later, Akash returned. 'He wake. You come with me.'

A sour smell met them at the door of the hut. In the semi-darkness, it was just possible to make out a low straw bed and the shape of a man lying on it. Closer to, it became clear that he was painfully thin; his gaunt face glistened with sweat. A woman who sat cross-legged near the bed stared at them and gave vent to an agitated torrent of words. She raised a thin brown arm and pointed at it then shook her fist.

'What's she saying?' asked de Silva, not understanding her accent even though she spoke in Tamil.

'She says she has sold her bangles to buy medicine for her husband, but he needs more, or he will die.'

De Silva steeled himself to go closer to the bed and saw the suppurating wound on the sole of one of Gooptu's feet. 'Ask her when he came home and how long he's been like this.'

'She remembers it was just before last poya day. He told them he had walked all the way. The wound on his foot was bleeding and full of dirt. The fever started soon afterwards,' said Akash after a brief conversation with the woman.

Poya day: the day of the full moon. If Gooptu had come home shortly before the last one, that was well before

Renshaw was found dead. He looked again at the wound on Gooptu's foot. The very thought of the man putting weight on it made him wince. Gooptu was certainly in no state to have walked all the way back to Nuala, broken into the factory and murdered Renshaw.

'I want to see his back. Ask her to turn him over.'

Akash spoke to the woman who started to cry and wring her hands. De Silva sighed and produced a few coins. She tucked them in a fold of her sari and wiped her eyes.

Gently, two men who had joined them in the hut turned Gooptu over. De Silva studied the skin on his back. There were a few welts, but they weren't deep and seemed to be healing a great deal more cleanly than his foot.

'Let him lie down again. Prasanna, give me the shirt.'

Prasanna pulled it out of the bag he carried and handed it to de Silva. Gooptu was fully awake now, his breathing shallow and his eyes darting around these strange faces in his hut.

De Silva held up the shirt. 'Does this belong to you?' he asked.

Gooptu shook his head. De Silva was inclined to believe him. The shirt was far too large for this emaciated man and much of the stain was in a different place to the welts on Gooptu's back.

'Did your master flog you?'

Gooptu nodded and muttered a curse.

'Do you know anything about his death?'

Gooptu's chest heaved. De Silva realised he was laughing. 'Dead?' he gasped at last. 'Good.' He turned his head and spat out a gobbet of phlegm then closed his eyes once more. He looked as if he was going to sleep.

There seemed to be no point questioning him any further. De Silva pulled out some more money. 'Tell the wife to buy salt to clean the wound and medicine for her husband's fever.'

Outside he breathed in a lungful of clean air with relief. As they followed Akash back along the jungle paths, doubts filled his mind. Now he had seen Gooptu, he no longer considered him an obvious suspect. At least he could tell Jane the man had been found and seemed likely to recover.

But what about the other workers? If any of them had broken into the factory and committed the crime to avenge Gooptu, finding out who it was would be like looking for a needle in a haystack. And if one of them was the murderer, why would they stay on at the plantation and take the risk of being unmasked, especially with the place's future so uncertain?

Perhaps Hebden was right. Experience showed that the most obvious explanation for a death was frequently the correct one. In other words, Renshaw had died of a heart attack; there was nothing more to it than that. After all, as well as now having no obvious suspect, he had found no murder weapon either. If Gooptu could be ruled out, and it seemed he could be, all that was left was vague suspicion.

He thought of Madeleine Renshaw and Tagore, of the grazes on Renshaw's body, and the unwashed teacup with the smell he couldn't place. When he made his report to Archie Clutterbuck, which he still had to do, he wasn't even sure he would mention them. With Renshaw dead, Clutterbuck would probably want the matter forgotten as soon as possible. Until he had something convincing to back up his theory that Renshaw had been murdered, he preferred to avoid giving the impression he was just being difficult.

CHAPTER 12

The organ's sonorous tones filled the church. A rustle like the wind in a grove of coconut trees accompanied it as the congregation rose to their feet.

Bearing the coffin on their shoulders, the pall bearers walked slowly to the table before the altar and set down their burden. Madeleine Renshaw, veiled in black, followed. Hamish, dressed in a dark suit and tie and a white shirt that made him look like a parody of a grown-up, clutched her hand. De Silva felt a stab of pity for the boy. Even if he hadn't been close to his stepfather, this death must remind him that he had lost his natural father. His home would be a sombre place for many months too.

The vicar stepped forward and spoke the opening words of the funeral service. Renshaw might not have been a popular man, thought de Silva, but almost every pew was full. From where he and Jane sat towards the back of the church, he surveyed the rows of bowed heads. Most of the planters in the area and their families were there and many of the Renshaws' household staff. Doctor Hebden sat in the same pew as the Clutterbucks.

The congregation remained standing to sing a hymn. De Silva, who was no singer, mumbled through it. The organist reached the final chords and they knelt to pray then the vicar called for a few moments of silence: a time for all those present to meditate on their memories of the departed. How many of those memories would be kindly? de Silva wondered and then felt ashamed.

A grating sound and footsteps distracted him. To his surprise, he saw Ravindra Tagore ease himself into one of the pews on the other side of the aisle. So, he hadn't returned to Colombo yet. But what was he doing here? He was the last person de Silva would have expected to want to pay his respects.

When the service ended the congregation followed the coffin to the churchyard where it was lowered into the grave and the vicar spoke the final prayers. Afterwards people stood in little knots and chatted, waiting for a decent interval to pass before moving on to the funeral lunch.

De Silva found himself beside the Clutterbucks.

'The nerve of the man!' Florence's chins wobbled and he realised that what she often reminded him of was a jungle fowl. 'After the accusations he made in that poor man's lifetime, you'd think he'd have the decency not to darken the church doors.'

'A bad business all round,' her husband growled. 'The sooner the fellow makes himself scarce, the better.'

Florence snorted and shot a glance across the churchyard at Tagore who was talking to Madeleine, but then her attention was distracted by the sight of someone she wanted to speak with. Husband in tow, she sailed off across the grass.

Jane sighed. 'I wish they weren't quite so harsh. I know it's strange that Tagore's here, especially as he said he was planning to go back to Colombo several days ago, but he behaved respectfully, and his intentions may be good.' She thought for a moment. 'He was talking to Madeleine. I wonder why he didn't mention her when I asked if he knew anyone in Nuala.'

'Perhaps he doesn't know her well,' said de Silva with a shrug. 'It would be natural to offer your condolences at a funeral. Speaking of which, there's David Leung, Renshaw's friend.'

'Madeleine certainly won't be pleased to see him. One thing she's told me is that she didn't like his influence over her husband. She hoped he might lose contact when they left Colombo, but he turned up again like the bad penny. Oh dear, he's going over to speak to her. Shall we go to her rescue?'

Tagore parted with Madeleine as they approached, acknowledging Leung with the briefest of nods as the two men passed each other. He stopped to greet the de Silvas with an uneasy smile.

'Good morning, Mr Tagore,' said Jane. 'Wasn't it a lovely service?'

'Yes, it was, Mrs de Silva.'

'I didn't realise you knew Mrs Renshaw.'

'We met once or twice in Colombo when her first husband was alive. Our acquaintance is very slight.'

'Are you staying for the lunch? I'd love to hear more about what you've been up to since my Colombo days.'

'I'm afraid I shall have to forgo the pleasure. I still have a great deal to do before I leave, so I must be on my way. It has taken me longer to settle my mother's affairs than I expected.' He made a little bow. 'It's been a pleasure to see you again.'

'You were very quiet, Shanti,' Jane whispered as Tagore walked away.

'I doubt he wanted to talk to me. Anyway, you're so much better at these awkward social encounters than I am.'

'I'm sure there's more to the situation with Madeleine than meets the eye.'

'Hmm.'

'Is that all you have to say?'

He decided not to mention the suspicion forming in his mind that not only did Tagore know Madeleine much better than he claimed, but also there might be a connection to Renshaw's death. As Tagore was still in Nuala, he'd find an opportunity to press him about who gave him the bloodstained shirt. It would be a good idea to tell him about the visit to Gooptu as well. It might convince him that de Silva was trying to help and make him more co-operative. People sometimes betrayed themselves if you won their trust.

Jane nudged him. 'Shanti?'

'What more *can* I say, my love?' he answered quickly. 'Anything else is surmise.'

She pinched his sleeve. 'Sometimes you're very provoking.'

'I'll try not to be in future.'

He offered her his arm. 'Ah, I see Madeleine has managed to extricate herself from David Leung's company without our assistance and people are starting to move on. Shall we go and find that lunch?'

CHAPTER 13

The telephone rang in the hall at Sunnybank and de Silva went to answer it. Jane's voice greeted him.

'How was the journey back to the plantation?' he asked.

'Very good thank you, dear. I must say, the Clutterbucks' car is most comfortable. Florence was needed at the Residence so Madeleine and I had it to ourselves.'

'Excellent.'

'I thought you might be at the police station.'

'I checked in there, but there was nothing urgent, so I came home.' If he was truthful, the funeral lunch organised by Florence Clutterbuck was sitting rather heavily on his stomach.

'What are you doing for the rest of the day?'

'I might read or do some paperwork.'

'Oh, if you're not too busy, I forgot my library books need returning. They're already overdue I'm afraid.'

'Then I'll save your ham and take them back.'

'Bacon, dear, bacon. I have a list of new ones to take out too if you don't mind.'

'Not at all.'

'Will you ring me tomorrow?'

'Of course.'

'I'd better go. I hear Madeleine calling. Goodbye, dear.'

'Save the bacon,' de Silva muttered. He must remember that.

Nuala's subscription library bore little resemblance to its counterpart at the Crown, but with its cluttered shelves and comfy seats it had a certain homely charm. He arrived half an hour before closing time and deposited Jane's stack of detective stories on the counter. The librarian left off shelving books and came to check them back in, removing the little slips of brown card tucked in the front covers.

He paid the small fine and handed her the list of books Jane wanted. She ran her eye down it and nodded. 'I think all of them are in, Inspector de Silva. Except this one,' she pointed, 'and Mrs De Silva doesn't say which cookery book she'd like.'

'She said something the other day about cake recipes. She's decided it's time to persuade our cook to be more adventurous.'

'Well, most of our cookery books should have a section on baking. We haven't many, but if you go past detective novels and turn left at history, you'll find what we have on the top shelf. Do you need my help?'

'Thank you, but I think I can manage.'

He found his way to the shelves where detective novels were kept and hunted for the titles Jane had listed. When he had located them all, he moved on to the place the librarian mentioned and studied the small selection of cookery books. Most of these tomes struck horror into his heart – recipes for English dishes of a more dismal nature than he had thought possible – but there were several recipes for cakes. One of them involving coconut and lime even looked quite appetising. The author of the book wrote that it was the perfect addition to afternoon tea.

Tea. De Silva scratched his chin. The loose tea and stained cup he had found in Renshaw's office were still in the trunk of the Morris. Preoccupied with following the lead to Gooptu – the lead which had led nowhere – he had done nothing about them. He placed the cookery book on top of his pile and went to look for a section on medicine. If he was right that the tea was pitta, it might be worthwhile expanding his knowledge about it.

The medical section was even slimmer than cookery, but there was one book entitled *Ayurvedic Medicine: a brief outline* by an Englishman, Doctor Oswald Scroop. Hebden had mentioned that some English medics took an interest in Ceylon's traditional herbal remedies.

A glance at the copyright page showed that the book was nearly fifty years old. The cover had faded from red to pink and presumably the book hadn't been opened for many years as some of the pages needed peeling apart, but it was better than nothing and luckily, he had a ticket to spare.

He took everything to the counter and waited while the librarian stamped the books out and worked her magic with more little slips of card. In the Morris he put the pile on the passenger seat and motored slowly home, enjoying the warm evening air.

Dinner was a briefer meal than usual. He never liked to linger over food when he ate alone. In any case, he wanted to learn what Dr Scroop had to teach him. He made himself comfortable in the drawing room with a glass of whisky at his elbow and began to read.

The good doctor's style was dry and somewhat turgid, but de Silva ploughed on, only occasionally finding that his eyelids drooped, and he had to stand up and walk about the room to refresh himself. Eventually, he reached the part where Scroop discussed the benefits and properties of pitta tea. From the doctor's description of what it contained, it seemed de Silva's sense of smell had not deceived him.

He continued reading. Most of the benefits of the tea that Scroop detailed were familiar to him. People drank it in order to balance their digestive systems, soothe the stomach and generally calm fevered temperament. It aided sleep and healed the skin. It relieved burning pains in the joints and cooled irritability. In addition to drinking the tea, there was also a list of foods to avoid. He ran his finger down them. They were foods that were pungent, sour, or salty; heat inducing foods like chilli and hot pepper; coffee, and some fruits and nuts – almonds in particular unless they had been peeled and well soaked.

He paused. The smell he hadn't been able to place in the tea, was it almond? He got up, fetched the box containing the tea and the cup that he had brought in from the car, and sniffed the tea carefully. He still detected rose, mint, liquorice, and coriander, but not almond. Raising the cup to his nostrils, he sniffed again. Did he imagine a faint smell of almonds? But why on earth would you put almonds in pitta tea if they were generally one of the foods to avoid?

He took the cup to the sideboard, picked up the soda syphon and squirted in a little soda, swilling it around to release the brownish residue. In his time in Colombo he had learnt a few things about poisons. Only one gave off the faint smell of bitter almonds.

In the garden the waning moon cast an eerie light, too dim to see by. He returned to the verandah, found one of the lanterns Jane liked to keep there and lit it. The trees stirred in the light wind as he walked along the flowerbeds until he found what he was looking for. It was a fat, horned slug. After a short tussle with his conscience, he bent down and poured some of the contents of the cup over it. Slowly, the creature's slimy body began to bubble and fizz; after a few moments, it was a shapeless mess.

He stood up and stared at the puddle of slime. He had been right to suspect foul play. Charles Renshaw hadn't died of heart failure. He had been poisoned with cyanide. Here was the murder weapon. Now he had to work out who had wielded it.

He turned over in his mind what his course of action should be. His conclusion was that it would be a good idea to find out more about David Leung's movements, and also Ravindra Tagore's.

CHAPTER 14

Constable Nadar was alone at the station when de Silva got there early the next morning.

'Hasn't Prasanna arrived yet?'

'He has, sir, but he left again to spend the morning looking for the owner of the ponies at the lake. He said you wanted to get on with it before there was an accident.'

'So I did.' He thought for a moment. If Prasanna had already been back to the Crown, he would have mentioned it or left a message. It wasn't really his fault if he hadn't pursued the matter. At the time he hadn't seen it as particularly important himself.

'I have to go out. If anyone calls, you'll have to deal with them, Nadar.'

'Yes, sir.'

His constable was becoming more confident, thought de Silva as he hurried out to the Morris and started the engine. A year ago he would have looked apprehensive at the suggestion.

He turned his mind to the matter in hand. Overnight a few doubts had crept in, but daylight had dispelled them. His gut feeling was still that it was too soon to involve anyone else, but he was sure that he had a murder investigation on his hands.

He drew up at the Crown, went to the reception desk and asked to see the manager in private. The man rose to his feet when de Silva entered his office. 'Good morning, Inspector. I hope nothing is amiss?'

'Nothing concerning the hotel, but I need some information about one of your guests.'

'I'm not sure we are at liberty—'

'You are if I'm making the inquiry in an official capacity and that is the case here.'

The manager looked crestfallen. 'Very well, Inspector. What do you want to know?'

'I understand you have a Mr David Leung staying at the hotel.'

'Yes. Mr Leung has been here – let me see – I believe it is ten days now.'

'What can you tell me about his movements?'

'Very little. He spends most of his days away from the hotel. I believe he often takes luncheon at the Empire Club.'

'And evenings?'

The manager shrugged. 'Occasionally he dines alone here. Otherwise I couldn't say.'

'What about last Saturday? The evening of the Hatton cricket match.'

'I shall have to enquire, Inspector. One moment, please.'

He picked up the telephone and spoke for a few moments then replaced the receiver. 'Mr Leung was not booked in for dinner that evening.'

'And what time did he return to the hotel?'

'I'm afraid we don't keep track of all our guests' movements, Inspector.'

De Silva ignored the tone. 'I imagine the night porter who was on duty might remember. I'd like to speak to him.'

The manager frowned. 'He will be sleeping in the staff quarters now.'

'Then he'll have to wake up. I won't keep him long.'

With a reluctant air, the manager led him along a maze of corridors, much narrower than those in the public area of the hotel. Heat and steam billowed from the kitchens they passed. De Silva glanced in and saw the cooks and kitchen boys stripped to their loincloths as they worked. The shouting of orders and clattering of pans was deafening.

A row of storerooms contained sacks of spices, rice, and other cereals as well as bottles of wines and spirits. Outside, crates of fruit and vegetables were being unloaded from carts and two men were shovelling a pile of refuse into a huge incinerator. Another pushed a cart loaded with soiled laundry into an open-fronted washhouse where women were scrubbing away on washboards or rinsing sheets in big tanks. Smells of soap and bleach drifted out, making de Silva's nostrils prickle.

They reached the shacks where the hotel staff lived, and the manager went to call the porter. The man emerged scratching his head and blinking at the sunshine. 'Many people came in late that night,' he said when de Silva questioned him and described Leung.

'Try and think. Mr Leung has a distinctive appearance – expensively dressed, very pale skin but jet-black hair. He would have driven up in a black Daimler.'

The man's bony hand rasped his chin. 'Yes, I remember now.'

'And what time was it?'

'Half past three. Maybe four o'clock.'

'You're sure it wasn't earlier?'

'Yes. It gets cold by then.' He grimaced. 'I don't forget that.'

'Thank you.'

De Silva dropped a few annas into the man's hand. 'Here's something for your trouble.'

The man grinned and took the money then ducked back into the shack.

'I hope that was satisfactory,' said the manager as they returned to the hotel.

'Perfectly, and I hope you understand that I rely on your discretion. My visit must remain confidential.'

'Inspector, everything that happens within the walls of this hotel is confidential.'

So, thought de Silva as he drove back to the station, Leung had arrived back at the hotel at the very least three and a half hours after he left the plantation. How could the journey have taken so long? Even though much of the road was poor and he had been driving in the dark, there were two and a half hours not accounted for. But then if Hebden was right and Renshaw died at about five o'clock, Leung was already back at the hotel by then.

Rickshaws and bullock carts jostled for space on the road as he neared the bazaar. The Morris came to a stop beside a stall where plucked fowls hung by their feet. The stallholder haggled with a buyer who was prodding a scrawny carcass. De Silva frowned. If it was cyanide that killed Renshaw, he would have died almost as fast as that fowl when its neck was wrung. Even if Leung had returned to the factory and the night watchman hadn't seen him do so, on Hebden's analysis, the facts didn't add up.

The bullock cart ahead of him pulled to one side and he edged the Morris past it. He needed to know more about Leung's movements that night. He also needed to talk to an old acquaintance who might be able to help him with Hebden's estimate of the time of Renshaw's death.

Back at the station, he made two telephone calls: one to the most respected hospital in Colombo, the other to the Crown Hotel. His old acquaintance was busy removing the appendix of a well-known Colombo businessman. David Leung was lunching at the Empire Club.

* * *

The Empire Club was housed in a building that was very much aware of its own importance. Constructed of brick as red as underdone beef, its roof was crowned with crenelated turrets that gave it a baronial air. A meticulously clipped, thorny shrub grew up the sides of the deep entrance porch as if to remind non-members that they entered on sufferance.

A liveried flunkey stepped forward the moment de Silva's foot landed on the thick, burgundy carpet. 'May I help you, Inspector?'

'Is Mr David Leung here?'

'I believe he is in for lunch. Is he expecting you?'

De Silva ignored the question. 'Please tell him I'd be obliged if he would spare me a few moments of his time.'

The click of cue on billiard ball and the hum of conversation drifted from a nearby room as de Silva waited. He surveyed the blackened-wood panelling that covered the walls to shoulder height. Above it they were hung with crimson paper embossed with a lighter pattern of flower motifs. An impressive chandelier composed of a huge iron hoop fitted with sconces containing the lamps dangled from a massive chain. The air was redolent of unquestioned privilege.

'Please come with me, Inspector,' the flunkey said on his return.

De Silva followed him to a room with a sign on the door marked "Private" and went in. David Leung greeted him with a handshake. 'A pleasure to see you again, Inspector. What can I do for you?' He nodded to the flunkey. 'Thank you. I'll ring the bell if we need anything.'

The door closed and the smile on Leung's face vanished. 'I hate to rush you, Inspector, but I have a guest lunching with me, and I expect him at any moment. Can we make this brief?'

'Certainly. Do you recall you told me that you left Charles Renshaw in his office at around midnight on the night of his death?'

'Yes.'

'Yet the night porter at the hotel remembers you returned to the hotel between half past three and four in the morning. The drive back from the plantation would take, say, an hour. Forgive me, but I must ask you what you were doing for the rest of the time.'

Not a flicker of disquiet disturbed Leung's impassive expression. 'There's no need to apologise, Inspector. The explanation is quite simple. As you know, the road up to Five Palms is very rough in many places. I'd been in a hurry to get my passengers back after the cricket. Charles was in a belligerent mood and poor Madeleine was becoming increasingly distressed. I decided that the best thing to do was separate them as soon as possible.

'I probably took a few too many chances on the bad stretches, especially where the road menders are working. Possibly I went over some broken glass or sharp scrap metal. On the way back to Nuala, I nearly lost control of the car and realised that I had a flat tyre. I stopped and tried to find help, but there was no one about. In the end I had to change to the spare wheel myself.'

He splayed the well-manicured fingers of one hand. 'Unfortunately for the occasion, my abilities don't lie in that direction, so it took me quite a while.'

'Do you remember what the time was when you stopped and where you were?'

'About half past twelve, and I was still a good five miles from the outskirts of town. I'm afraid I can't be more precise than that. There were no particular landmarks to distinguish the spot from any other around there.'

Inwardly de Silva acknowledged that was true of much of that road.

'You may recall it rained heavily that night. I decided against trying to walk back to town and leave dealing with the car until morning. By the time the rain stopped, no other cars had come by. As I say, it took me quite a while to change the wheel after that. I was too tired to notice precisely what time I reached the hotel, but more likely nearer half past three than four o'clock.'

'Which tyre was it?'

'I hope I'm not being interrogated, Inspector.'

'Just getting the facts straight, sir.'

'The offside rear.'

He glanced at the gold watch protruding from the cuff of his immaculate white shirt.

'One last thing, which garage did you use to repair the tyre?'

Leung's eyes narrowed then the smile returned. 'Gopallawa Motor Repairs. They were recommended by the manager, and I found them satisfactory.'

De Silva thanked him and left. On the way back to the station, he mulled over what Leung had told him. It would be easy enough to check with the garage whether they had mended a punctured tyre. Leung had given the reason for the delay without hesitation, and it was plausible that the car would have been hard to control. On the other hand, the chances of verifying that there were skid marks at the spot were virtually nil.

At the station Constable Nadar was eating a large bowl of dahl. He quickly swallowed his mouthful. 'Sorry, sir, my wife is visiting her mother today, so I brought in my lunch.'

'That's alright, I'll be going home for mine in a moment. Have there been any calls?'

'Only one, sir, the assistant to Doctor Bruyn. He said the doctor is available now until five o'clock if you wish to call back.'

He pushed a piece of paper across the desk. 'I wrote down the number.'

De Silva folded the paper and put it in his pocket. He would go home to Sunnybank for lunch and ring Bruyn from there. Before he left the station, he telephoned Gopallawa Motor Repairs, but the manager was out. He left a message that he would ring again later.

He ate a solitary meal on the verandah at Sunnybank and washed it down with a stiff whisky and soda. He rarely drank alcohol during the day, but today he needed something to sharpen his brain. Could Hebden be wrong about the time when Renshaw died? If so, was it possible that Leung had returned to the factory unbeknown to the night watchman and got in, quite possibly in the way Prasanna had demonstrated?

A woodpecker landed on the jacaranda tree and started to hammer at the bark searching for insects. The beautiful flame-backed bird was one of de Silva's favourites, but he hardly glanced at it.

Why would Leung want to kill Renshaw? They were, apparently, friends. Close enough for Renshaw to ask for Leung's help with his financial problems. In one of Jane's detective novels, Leung might have planned his friend's death with a view to stepping into his shoes with his widow and the plantation, but this wasn't one of her novels. Leung seemed to be aware of the burden of debt on the plantation. Why would he see any advantage in taking it over? Jane was convinced that Madeleine's professed dislike of Leung was genuine too. The likelihood that they were involved in a conspiracy to murder her husband was very remote.

He pondered Madeleine's state of mind. She had been unhappy with her husband, but that wasn't automatically a motive for murder. If it were, half the husbands in the world would be in danger sometimes.

But what if Leung had nothing to do with it? What if Madeleine and Tagore were lovers? Jane might be right that there was more between them than they were admitting. It was the most plausible explanation that the poison had been administered to Renshaw while he was in his office.

Drunk and half asleep, he probably hadn't realised what was happening.

Yet even if Madeleine had been responsible for making him drink the tea – pretending it was a restorative for example – how had he got to the withering tank? He remembered the bruising and scratches on Renshaw. His body had probably been dragged along the passage before being bundled into the tank. A slight woman like Madeleine would never have the strength to do that. Tagore, however, would be capable of it.

He put his head in his hands and pressed his fingers against his temples. One thing at a time: when, and if, David Leung was eliminated, that would be the time to turn his attention to Ravindra Tagore.

The sound of the telephone bell drifted from the hall. It stopped and a few moments later a servant came to the verandah doors. 'Gopallawa Motor Repairs, master.'

The wicker chair creaked as de Silva hauled himself out of it and went to take the call. He explained what he wanted to know and waited while the manager consulted his invoice book.

'Yes, Mr Leung's Daimler was here for a repair at the beginning of the week, sir.'

'What was the work you did?'

'A repair to a punctured tyre.'

De Silva thanked him and replaced the receiver. Now to speak to Doctor Bruyn. So far Leung's story rang true, but it would be valuable to know what Bruyn thought of Doctor Hebden's conclusions on the time of Renshaw's death.

* * *

'Shanti de Silva! This is an unexpected pleasure. It's been too long since we met. Tell me, what can I do for you?'

'The pleasure is all mine, Doctor Bruyn. If you have no objection, I'd be grateful for your professional advice on a matter I have in hand.'

'I'll do my best.'

Briefly, de Silva described how Renshaw's body had been found and the conclusion Hebden had come to about the time of his death.

The characteristic rumbling laugh de Silva remembered rolled out of the receiver. He pictured Bruyn's broad, genial face under the mane of grey hair. The doctor came from Dutch Burgher stock and had an imposing presence that endeared him to his privileged patients.

'I aim to keep my patients alive, de Silva. Fortunately, more often than not I succeed, so I don't have a great deal of expertise in that area, but then again most medical men have even less. It doesn't surprise me that your Doctor Hebden's analysis is somewhat crude.'

De Silva reached for a notepad and pen as Bruyn continued. 'This is fairly new science. Most of the work done so far has been in America. The academic papers I've read indicate that in cases where no one else was present to confirm it, it's not enough to take the rectal temperature and apply a linear formula in order to establish the time of a death. After death, bodies cool – or indeed warm – until they reach the temperature of the air around them. The rule of thumb is that this process takes place at the rate of one and a half degrees per hour, but that takes no account of many influential factors.'

'For example?'

'The deceased's physique for one. An overweight person cools more slowly than one who is thin. Fat is an excellent insulator. The presence of alcohol in the body may have a bearing on the rate of cooling as well. You also need to consider where the body was found. If it was in a cool room but wrapped in excessively warm clothing, the rule of thumb is less helpful than if the body was naked or lightly clothed. Of course, once the body has reached ambient temperature, none of this is any use.'

Bruyn paused. 'Does that help?'

'Indeed it does. Thank you.'

'Good. I doubt there's any further light I can shed, but if anything occurs to you, I'd be happy to try.'

De Silva thought quickly. On his principle of checking every detail, there was one more thing and it was a matter a doctor might be able to help with. Namely that if the bloodstained shirt didn't belong to Gooptu, who did it belong to? It was a long shot but if the blood type or even just the length of time the shirt had been stained could be identified, it might help in some way.

'By all means send it down to me,' said Bruyn when de Silva asked him. 'I'm not sure if it will be possible to tell anything. It may depend on how old the stain is, but the boys in the lab might be able to help. I must say you intrigue me, de Silva. I won't ask you to divulge any secrets now but one day you must tell me what this is all about.'

De Silva thanked him again and they said goodbye. He went back into the garden and paced the lawn. Precision might still elude him, but the conversation had been very useful. It had exposed Hebden's diagnosis as simplistic and possibly wrong.

He consulted his watch. It was only three o'clock. There was plenty of time to visit the Five Palms plantation. Even if he could rule out David Leung, it would be interesting to find out anything Madeleine knew about him and her husband's financial affairs in general.

In any case, he missed Jane.

CHAPTER 15

The sun glinted on the surface of the lake as he drove by. For a change there were no ponies about. Maybe Prasanna was having some success after all. He put his foot down and the speedometer needle crept up.

He was still resolved not to burden Jane with his suspicions for the present. She had enough to do consoling Madeleine Renshaw, and anyway numerous questions remained unanswered in his own mind. Smiling, she came to meet him across the bungalow's lawn. 'Shanti dear. I'm so glad to see you.'

They exchanged a kiss. 'And I you. How's everything going here?'

'She's started to talk a little more, but oh dear, Shanti, she's so worried about the future. She keeps saying she doesn't know how she can stay on here and if it's not possible, where will she and Hamish go?'

'I'm afraid she has good reason to be worried. Does she have any family?'

'Only some distant relatives in England. She doesn't relish the prospect of appealing to them.'

'That's understandable.'

'Shanti, I'd like to tell her that if she has to go, she and Hamish are welcome to stay with us for a while. I've grown very fond of them both.'

'Of course.'

He hoped his voice didn't betray the uncertainty he felt. If Madeleine Renshaw was a conspirator, her future would not be in her own hands.

'Has she said anything about the financial troubles here? I noticed some old photographs in Renshaw's office. It looked from those as if the plantation was a prosperous concern once.'

'Madeleine said there was a long-drawn-out legal dispute over who was to inherit. The deceased owner was Charles's distant cousin. Eventually, the case was resolved in Charles's favour, but the plantation was neglected while it went on. When they came here there was so much to do. Old tea bushes needed to be grubbed out and the fields replanted. A lot of the machinery was rusting or needing repair.'

They heard footsteps and Hamish ran down the stairs from the verandah. He stopped when he saw de Silva, who smiled encouragingly. 'Have you forgotten me already? How's that bird of yours?'

Hamish came the rest of the way and took Jane's hand. This whole business was bound to shake the boy's confidence, thought de Silva.

'He has to live in his cage,' Hamish said sadly. 'Mamma says she doesn't like him to be free.'

'But you can go and see him as often as you like,' said Jane kindly.

Hamish's face brightened. 'Can I go now?'

'Of course.'

'So Jacko had to be banished after all, did he?' asked de Silva as the little boy scampered away.

'Yes, he did. His language really is appalling, and it seems to set Madeleine's nerves even more on edge than they already are.'

'Where has he been banished to?'

'A cage in the kitchen yard.'

'Perhaps a spell there will reform him.'

'I doubt it,' Jane said acerbically. 'If he has to come to us, he might end up in the pot.'

De Silva chuckled. 'That's not very charitable of you, my love.'

'It's not meant to be. Ah, here comes Madeleine.'

As she greeted de Silva, he thought how frail she looked. 'It's so kind of you to spare Jane,' she said. 'I don't know what I would have done without her these last few days.'

'You and Shanti sit down,' said Jane. 'I'll go and tell the servants to bring us out some tea.'

Madeleine squeezed her hand and gave her a sad, self-deprecating smile. 'Thank you. I'm not a very good hostess at the moment.'

'No one expects you to be, my dear.'

Jane went inside. Madeleine hesitated then she spoke in a low voice. 'I imagine Jane's told you about our situation, Inspector. Charles left me with a pile of debts. I've no experience of business and I shall probably be forced to sell the plantation.'

'I'm very sorry to hear it. Jane and I were talking just now. You and Hamish would be most welcome to stay with us at Sunnybank until you decide what to do.'

'You're both very kind.' She blinked and wiped her eyes.

'Did you have any idea of your late husband's financial problems?' he asked gently.

'I guessed all wasn't well.' She gestured to the bunga-low's shabby exterior and the garden's unkempt shrubs and trees. 'Charles would get so angry if I suggested making any improvements. But I didn't realise how bad the situation was.' She dabbed her eyes again. 'If only he'd talked to me, but then Charles and I didn't talk very much.'

'Did he ever mention a company called Asian Ventures?'

'Do you mean the one he owed most of the money to? No, I only heard about them after Charles died.' She frowned and was silent for a moment before she spoke again. 'David Leung's told me he'll try to help, but he warned I should be prepared for them to foreclose.'

Jane returned and sat down. She laid a hand on Madeleine's arm. 'I know it's hard but try not to distress yourself, my dear. Things have a way of working out in the end and you have Hamish. He will be a comfort to you.'

Madeleine gave a watery smile. 'In the beginning, I thought Charles and I could be happy together.'

'Of course you did.'

A squawk made Madeleine start. She gripped the arm of her chair and de Silva saw her knuckles whiten. 'How did that bird get out? Hamish! Come here.'

The little boy ran across the lawn. 'I didn't mean to let him out, Mamma. I only opened the door a little way to put a piece of mango in for him.'

He put his right hand to his mouth and sucked the knuckles. De Silva saw a streak of blood. 'He pecked me, and I let the door go by mistake.' He scowled. 'He hated being in that cage.'

Glorying in his freedom, Jacko took off from his perch among the flame-red flowers of an African tulip tree and flew in a big circle over the lawn. He landed on the grass and sidled towards the verandah, tilting his head to one side, and watching them with knowing eyes. 'Bastard!' he muttered. 'Bastard lawyer!'

Madeleine jumped up and ran at him, clapping her hands and shouting. With an offended shriek, he took off and soared into the treetops. Madeleine stood with upraised hands as if she had turned to stone.

Hamish burst into tears. 'You frightened him, Mamma! You frightened him! He'll never come back.'

Madeleine seemed to shrink as she turned to her son and held out her arms. 'Hamish, I'm sorry.'

'No! You're not sorry. I hate you.'

Jane got up. 'Hamish, you mustn't speak to your mother like that. Apologise at once.'

The boy stared at his feet. His face was scarlet as he mumbled the words.

'That's better. We'll go for a little walk and see if we can find him, shall we?'

Hamish put his hand in hers and they walked away towards the tall trees at the end of the garden. Madeleine hid her face in her hands. When she looked up again, her cheeks were wet. 'I'm so ashamed. You must think I've gone mad. It's my nerves. I can't stand that creature's noise.'

'There's no need to apologise. I'm sure the bird will come back, and order will be restored.'

She didn't reply.

'I expect you'd like some peace and quiet. I'll find Jane and say goodbye.'

She gave him a wan smile. 'Thank you for being so kind.'

He found Hamish and Jane still searching. 'You see what I mean?' she asked in a whisper. 'Poor girl, this is all so hard for her. I'd planned to come home soon, but perhaps I should stay a few more days.'

'Why not see how she is tomorrow? Let's talk in the morning.'

On the driveway he heard a long whistle followed by a stream of angry chatter. Perched on a wall, Jacko fluffed out his feathers and fixed him with a malevolent eye. 'Get out, bitch,' he squawked. 'Bastard!'

'If I were you, I'd make myself scarce for a while, Jacko.'

'Bastard!' Jacko riposted triumphantly. He let out a volley of sound like machine gun fire.

De Silva put his fingers in his ears. By the heavens, the bird was loud. He was surprised no one had come around from the garden.

Apparently delighted with his victory, Jacko preened then recommenced his imitation of a machine gun. Or was it? The noise was more ta-ta-ta than rat-a-tat, de Silva thought. The bird was a mimic. Of course it didn't understand the words it said. But they did reveal what it had heard. 'What are you trying to say, Jacko?' he asked. 'Ta-ta-ta?'

Jacko pecked at the creeper climbing over the wall then raised his head once more. 'Bastard,' he chuntered. 'Ta… tag… ah!'

So, it sounded like Madeleine and her husband had quarrelled over Tagore. What inference could he draw from that?

The roar of an engine sent Jacko fluttering up into a tree. De Silva turned to see the black Daimler sweep into the driveway. Leung nodded as he climbed out and, after a brief exchange of civilities, walked around to the garden.

One had to admire his self-possession, thought de Silva. It was as if there had never been a less than amicable exchange between them. Leung's visit wouldn't help Madeleine's peace of mind. It would be interesting to know what was said. Perhaps Jane would be able to enlighten him in the morning.

Leung had parked his car next to the Morris. As de Silva walked around the back of the Daimler, he saw that the bent spokes he had noticed before were still there. They were on the offside rear, where Leung said he had sustained the puncture. A pity that with such a fine car, he hadn't asked the garage to repair the damage when they fixed the tyre. If it had been the Morris, he certainly would have done so.

On the drive home his mind seethed with a jumble of thoughts. He told the servants to bring him a simple dahl and curry and ate a hasty meal. Afterwards he retired to his study where the fire had been lit. The cosy warmth and the food calmed him. Sitting at his desk, he found a large piece of paper and turned on the lamp. In bold letters, he wrote down four names: Gooptu, Leung, Tagore, and Madeleine. Then as an afterthought he added one more: Charles Renshaw.

He'd deal with Renshaw first. He hadn't yet considered the possibility that Renshaw had taken his own life.

He put down his pen, laced his fingers and rested his chin on them. Renshaw wouldn't be the first man driven to suicide by debt. Cyanide killed quickly. Many suicides had chosen to use it. Yet people rarely killed themselves without leaving some kind of farewell message. Then there were the bruises and abrasions. Hebden's theory that Renshaw had fallen didn't convince him. Those marks would be more likely to be concentrated at specific points like the knees or the chin. The marks on Renshaw's body were spread out. He hesitated then put a line through Renshaw's name.

Gooptu was next. He was the least likely of them all. He had reason to hate Renshaw, but the injury to his foot was clearly genuine. How could he have left his village in such a poor state of health? How too would he have had the money to buy the poison? Another line.

On to Leung. Was there something he was missing there? Leung's story about why he was delayed in returning to the hotel was plausible, but suppose Hebden was wrong about the time of death being five o'clock? Leung could have bribed the night watchman to say he had left the factory at a different time to when he really had. Perhaps he should go and question the watchman again? Maybe someone at the labour lines had noticed he had more money to spend than usual. That was a job for Prasanna. He'd mentioned taking the children a new cricket ball. A good excuse for a visit.

He circled Madeleine and Tagore's names and joined them with a line. None of what he knew so far amounted to evidence that would stand up in court, but it was pretty clear from the afternoon when he and Jane had seen them at the lake that Tagore was lying about the extent of their acquaintance. He was also sure that they were the couple he had glimpsed at the cricket match and Jacko's chatter provided further proof there was something between them.

If Madeleine and Tagore were in love, they certainly had a motive for wanting to be rid of Renshaw. Madeleine had the most obvious opportunity to get into the factory. It wouldn't be easy for a woman to get through that window, but she could probably find out where Renshaw kept spare keys. She would need to pass the night watchman to use the main door, however. There were other problems as well. How would she obtain the poison in secret, or haul Renshaw's body into the tank?

No, if Madeleine was involved, it had to have been with Tagore's help. Tagore was the key; he needed to find him.

He stretched and rolled his shoulders to ease them. There was nothing more he could do tonight. He might as well go to bed. Tomorrow, Tagore. There'd been no news about Asian Ventures from his old friend in Colombo either. About time he chased that up.

CHAPTER 16

He passed a restless night, disrupted by the distant sound of firecrackers. Strange how loud they were in the night. Like gunshots even if they were miles away. Early birds twittered in the garden by the time he slept deeply, and he didn't wake until half past eight. He pushed his feet into his slippers and reached for his paisley robe. The telephone rang in the hall, and he heard one of the servants answer it.

'It's the memsahib, sahib.' The man handed him the receiver. Jane's voice sounded troubled.

'I saw Leung arrive just as I left,' de Silva said. 'Did his visit upset her?'

'Not particularly. He didn't stay long. I'm afraid it's worse than that. That wretched bird was found dead this morning. Poor Hamish is so upset.'

'Oh dear, what happened?'

'We're not sure. Madeleine got up early, she said she hadn't slept well. Jacko was lying dead on the lawn covered in blood. Probably he came back wanting to be fed and a wild animal got him. Madeleine didn't want Hamish to see him, so she told one of the servants to bury the body at the bottom of the garden straight away. It's all very unfortunate. If only Madeleine hadn't scared Jacko away as she did, it might never have happened.'

De Silva decided not to mention what he had heard Jacko say on the driveway. It was still better to keep his suspicions to himself, even from Jane. 'How much longer will you stay?' he asked.

'Madeleine insists I come home on Monday as I planned. She says she feels better, and Florence Clutterbuck has been telephoning asking us both to visit the Residence for the day. You don't need to fetch us. Florence is sending the official car and we can drop off my luggage at Sunnybank then go on. They'll bring me back in the evening.'

'Won't Madeleine find it a bit of an ordeal?'

'She says not, but I must admit I'm surprised. Last night she was still saying she might have to tell Florence she wasn't feeling well enough to go, yet this morning, she seems determined. To tell the truth, it's probably for Hamish's sake. He loves that dog of Archie Clutterbuck's. It might cheer him up to see it.'

It would be good to have Jane back, he thought as he shaved. He hoped he hadn't been unfair in not telling her that he now suspected he was dealing with a murder. She was discreet, but if she was with Madeleine all the time, even she might let slip something it was too early to reveal.

He rinsed his face and towelled it dry, mulling over their conversation. It did seem very convenient that the delinquent Jacko was no more. And somewhat unlikely that such a crafty bird would fall victim to a wild animal. There was something about the story that didn't fit. He must try to find a way of verifying it.

* * *

He spent a quiet Sunday alone. In the evening Jane telephoned again. He felt a traitor for not taking her into his confidence, but he kept his resolve. The atmosphere at the bungalow had improved a little throughout the day, she said. Hamish was excited about the trip to Nuala.

'Oh, and Florence wants me to stay for the evening.'

She laughed and he pictured her rolling her eyes. 'She's organised one of her soirées. We're to have readings and a string quartet. It won't be a late evening. Do you mind if I accept? You don't have to come.'

De Silva felt relieved. He liked music and literature, but an evening spent trussed up in a starched shirt and stiff collar was not his idea of the best way to enjoy them. 'Of course not. But what will Madeleine and her boy do afterwards?'

'They'll stay at the Residence. Florence insists it will be no trouble. In fact, she's persuaded Madeleine to be their guest for a few days. There's a charity luncheon at the Crown and she might like to see the new film at the Casino. It's certainly a change of heart on Madeleine's part – as if she suddenly can't wait to be away from this place. I'm sure it will do her the world of good to get out of herself. It might make her stronger for when she has to deal with the problem of what to do about the plantation.'

De Silva's head ached. His wife was so full of plans for helping Madeleine Renshaw. He dreaded being the one who might have to dash them.

* * *

When Monday morning came, he left for the police station without taking his usual morning walk around the garden. Sergeant Prasanna jumped to his feet as he came in. 'Good news, sir! The owner of four of the ponies is found and I hope to know who the others belong to very soon.'

'You'll have to leave that for the moment, Prasanna. I've more important things for you to do. Have you taken that cricket ball you promised to the children at the Renshaw plantation's labour lines?'

'Not yet, sir. There hasn't been time.'

'Get over there today. Start up another game if you need to and get the workers talking. I want you to find out if anyone has been noticed having more money to spend than usual. Particularly the watchman who was there on the night Renshaw died.'

A puzzled expression came over Prasanna's face.

'You'd better fetch Constable Nadar. I need to explain the situation to both of you. Where is he?'

'In the yard, burning those old papers you wanted destroyed, sir.'

'Well, hurry up and call him in.'

De Silva paced the room as he waited for them. Nadar came in fumbling with the top button of his uniform tunic; he wiped a smut from his nose.

'The fact is,' de Silva said briskly, 'I've reached the conclusion that Charles Renshaw didn't die of a heart attack. He was murdered.'

Constable Nadar's eyes widened. 'How, sir?'

'Cyanide: administered in a cup of pitta tea.'

Prasanna frowned. 'But we saw in the village that Gooptu was too sick to walk and anyway, he has no money for such things. Neither do the other workers.'

'I don't think it was revenge on the part of Gooptu or any of the other workers, although I admit that was my first reaction. No, my suspects are quite different. One of them is David Leung. As you know, he was with Renshaw that night. He claimed he left at about midnight and the night watchman corroborated his story, but he didn't reach the Crown Hotel before half past three.'

'Do you think the night watchman may have been bribed to give the wrong time then, sir?' Prasanna asked.

'Very good, Sergeant, you're thinking. We have to consider the possibility. I've interviewed Mr Leung and he has an explanation for why it took him three and a half hours to drive from the plantation to the Crown, but we only have his and the night watchman's word for the time he left.'

'But I read the report Doctor Hebden sent in. It certified that Mr Renshaw died at five o'clock.'

'It's not as simple as that, Sergeant. Doctor Hebden may be incorrect.'

'You said *one* of the suspects, sir?'

'Yes.'

De Silva hesitated. For the present he wouldn't mention Madeleine. If he was wrong about her, it would be unforgivable to have besmirched a lady's name. It wasn't necessary to extend the same courtesy to Tagore, however. 'The other is the lawyer who laid the complaint against Renshaw: Ravindra Tagore.'

His mind went back to the break-in at the Ayurvedic shop, and he wondered if he had dismissed it too soon. But then he decided not to reopen the matter yet. It was perfectly possible that the killer had obtained the tea by legitimate means. He turned to Nadar. 'I want you to go to the Ayurvedic shops in town and find out if they've sold any pitta tea in the last week or so.'

Nadar looked crestfallen. Nuala had many such places.

'Prasanna will help you when he comes back. If they have, find out whether any of the customers were new ones. I imagine most of the shops know their regulars.'

After they'd gone de Silva telephoned the Nuala Hotel. 'Mr Tagore left us last Friday, sir,' the receptionist said.

'The day before the Hatton cricket match?'

'Yes.'

'Do you have a forwarding address?'

'I'm afraid not, sir.'

Ending the call, de Silva frowned. It was clear that Tagore had stayed in Nuala after he checked out of the hotel. Why hadn't he remained there? Was it because he didn't want anyone to know his movements? He scratched his chin.

He'd have to find another way of tracking the lawyer down, but what could that be? Then he remembered why Tagore had been at the church when he and Jane met him. He'd mentioned that his mother had recently been buried there. The vicar might know where he was to be found.

* * *

De Silva locked up and drove to St George's. Away from the bustle of the Nuala streets, the churchyard drowsed in the sunshine. Gravestones reared up from the long grass, the newer ones straight, the rest at tipsy angles. A few graves had low metal railings around them, but most were simple rectangular mounds of earth. Fresh flowers decorated the plots where the friends and families of the deceased still visited the graveyard.

De Silva walked up and down the rows until he found Tagore's mother's plot. It was in the shade of a cherry tree, a scattering of whose fragile white petals had fallen and caught in the grass. There was no headstone yet, just a wooden cross with a plaque giving her name and the dates. Someone, Tagore probably, had put a bunch of wild flowers in a small jug there. De Silva smelled their sweetness.

There was no one about so he went into the church, but it was also deserted. He would have to call at the vicarage. He found the gate in the corner of the churchyard and went down an uneven path between camellia and rhododendron bushes.

The vicarage was a low stone building with pretensions to Victorian Gothic architecture. The windows were set in pointed arches decorated with carvings and the door was a massive piece of oak, hinged and studded with iron. He rang the bell and eventually a servant answered the door. 'Please tell Reverend Peters that Inspector de Silva is here to see him.'

The man waggled his head and went away. A few moments later, the vicar emerged from his study. He looked rather bemused. De Silva was not surprised. He rarely accompanied Jane to church. He might as well get straight to the point.

'Ravindra Tagore,' the vicar said thoughtfully when asked the question. 'He was in Nuala recently to attend his mother's funeral, but I only met him at the service. All the arrangements were seen to by the undertakers. But come in, come in. I may have something in my records. If not, I'll give you the undertakers' name and you might like to enquire there.'

De Siva followed him into a dimly lit, cluttered room that smelled of peppermints and waited while the vicar riffled through papers. At last he shook his head. 'I'm afraid not, but the undertakers were Baileys in Hatton.'

'I know them. Thank you.'

'Are you a friend of Mr Tagore's?'

'An acquaintance. I have some legal business I would like to discuss with him.'

'His mother was a charming lady. She came to church every Sunday until her final illness. I was very glad to be able to visit her in hospital several times before she died.'

He accompanied de Silva to the door. 'A sad business about Charles Renshaw,' he observed. 'I understand your wife is a friend of his widow's. I don't know Mrs Renshaw well myself. She comes to church but rarely takes part in our other activities. I suppose their plantation is rather remote.'

De Silva thanked him and returned to the station. When he tried to telephone the undertakers, however, the line to Hatton was down. He looked at his watch. There was time to drive there if he left straight away.

* * *

The drive was a pleasant one, but to his annoyance, when he arrived, he found the premises closed. He waited for ten minutes in case someone returned then another idea occurred to him. The Registry of Births and Deaths in Nuala would issue him with Mrs Tagore's death certificate which would show her last address. Tagore might have gone there, or there might at least be something – a letter or an address book perhaps – showing where he lived. He wished he had thought of that before driving all this way.

He reached the Town Hall in time to fill in the two forms required and pay the fee. The clerk handed him a receipt and suggested he return the next day. Feeling irritable, de Silva went back to the station. It had been a wasted day. Another evening alone stretched before him.

He was on the station doorstep with his key in the lock when there was a squeak of brakes and Prasanna jumped off his bicycle.

'Did you find out anything?'

Prasanna shook his head. 'No one there has been spending more money than usual, sir. In fact, they were all very subdued. The manager is still sending pluckers out into the fields, but no one knows whether the leaves they collect will ever go to the auctions. Some of the workers have left to find other jobs.'

'I see. Thank you, Prasanna. You may as well get off home.'

CHAPTER 17

Jane returned home from Florence Clutterbuck's musical evening later than she expected – the string quartet had played several encores – so, luckily for de Silva, it wasn't hard for him to hold to his resolve to keep his own counsel.

Overnight an idea for checking whether the story of Jacko's death was true had come to him. After breakfast he left for the police station as usual then drove out to Five Palms with Prasanna. Just before the last stretch of the road to the bungalow, he turned into a narrow lane he had noticed on his last visit. As he hoped, it brought them close to the rear boundary of the bungalow's garden.

A belt of jungle separated it from the lane. He went ahead of Prasanna, picking his way carefully, lifting ferns and creepers with a stick as he walked, watchful for any slithering movement that would indicate there was a snake. The air buzzed with the sound of insects; the sun beat on his back.

Their walk ended at a dense stand of coconut palms and a broken-down wire fence. They climbed over it, edged past the tall tree trunks, and began to comb the ground, looking for a patch that had been recently disturbed.

'I think it's here, sir,' Prasanna called softly after a few minutes.

De Silva went over and studied the place. Brushwood and creepers had been cut back from an area a few feet square, exposing the densely packed red earth. In a smaller square in the centre, the earth was powdery.

Prasanna pushed the sharp edge of the spade he had been carrying into the ground. After two shovel loads, he struck something solid. He loosened the soil round about then knelt down and scooped it away until he unearthed a wooden box of the kind used to store tea. He opened it and lifted out a bundle.

Wrapped inside was Jacko; his plumage had lost its sheen and his eyes were closed. De Silva picked him up. Apart from the blood caking the feathers on his breast, there was no sign of injury. If he had been caught by a predator, it must have been scared away before it had time to do much damage. He held the bird up to the light and checked him over again. The blood looked thicker on one part of the breast. 'Do you have a knife, Sergeant?'

'Yes, sir.'

De Silva crouched down and laid Jacko on the ground. Carefully, he parted some of his feathers and felt for the flesh, then he took the knife and put the tip of the blade into the gory mess. A small twist and a fragment of flattened metal popped out.

'That's the first time I've come across a wild animal that knows how to use a gun,' he remarked. He put the fragment in his pocket. 'Wrap him up and put him back, Prasanna. Try to fill in the hole as if nothing's been disturbed.'

'Yes, sir.'

They drove back to Nuala, threading through bullock carts and rickshaws as they neared the centre of town. He stopped at the Town Hall to collect the death certificate then dropped Prasanna at the station and set off for the address where Tagore's mother had lived.

* * *

The lane up to the late Mrs Tagore's home was steep with high banks on either side. He put the Morris into second gear and the car crawled up, protesting. Ferns grew on the banks with a sprinkling of wild flowers among them. Butterflies flitted from one bright clump to another.

Weeds had colonised the gravelled splay in front of the bungalow. At the gate, the perfume of a magnificent angel's trumpet shrub met him. There were roses under the bungalow windows, in sore need of pruning but still producing a good show of crimson flowers. A border to one side of the building displayed some of the rarer shrubs and plants de Silva knew. A lover of gardens had once lived here.

On the opposite side to the shrub border stood a garage. He glimpsed a black Austin parked inside and immediately recalled Tagore's mother. He had seen her sometimes on his occasional visits to church with Jane. A grizzled chauffeur, almost as elderly as she was, had always driven her up to the lych-gate and dropped her off. She had been a petite, elegant lady, dressed in the western-style fashions he recalled seeing in his youth. Whatever the weather, a fur tippet had always been draped around her neck. Her outfits were usually complemented by numerous ropes of pearls.

No one answered when he rang the bell, so he walked around to the garden side of the bungalow. At first, he thought that the man hacking dead branches off an old apple tree with a machete must be the gardener, then he realised it was Tagore. He wore the traditional sarong, and his chest was bare. De Silva observed the broad shoulders and well-muscled arms. Tagore was also considerably taller than he was. If it came to a fight, he hoped he wouldn't regret not bringing Prasanna or Nadar.

He was a few feet away before Tagore heard him. He turned and pushed a lock of wavy black hair out of his eyes.

'Good morning, Inspector. This is a surprise. What can I do for you?'

The words were civil, but Tagore's expression was wary and unsmiling. De Silva glanced at the keen edge of the machete and his mouth dried. 'I have a few questions I'd like to ask you, Mr Tagore.'

'Then you'd better come inside.'

The bungalow's interior was attractive and filled with light. Elegant brocade curtains hung at the windows of the room into which Tagore took him. The furniture was rosewood and there were watercolours of flowers and gardens on the walls.

Tagore picked up an old towel draped over the back of a sofa and wiped the sweat from his face and torso. 'Will you excuse me while I fetch a shirt?'

'Certainly.'

While he waited, de Silva looked around the room. There were a few papers out on a desk, but they were merely letters of condolence and the undertakers' bill, nothing of any interest.

He studied the silver-framed photographs on the rosewood piano. In one of them Mrs Tagore stood beside a distinguished-looking man. From the resemblance, he was presumably Tagore's father. They were both smiling, their heads almost touching, dressed for some special occasion. Other photographs showed a handsome little boy who must be Tagore playing with a variety of large dogs. There were also photographs of racehorses, and one of the Austin in the garage.

De Silva picked it up and studied it. At the bottom of the picture, the words *Austin 10hp 1912* were inscribed in white.

'You take an interest in cars, Inspector?'

Tagore had come back into the room. Dressed in western-style trousers now, he was tucking his shirt tails into the waistband. He seemed more relaxed, but a glimmer of wariness was still in his eyes.

'Have done since I was a young man.'

'Are you in the market for a new one? I'll give you a good price. I have no use for a car in Colombo. It's in excellent condition. My father was a careful driver. He was very fond of horseracing and he and my mother liked to go to the races at Kandy sometimes, but otherwise they only used the car for short journeys. After he died, my mother's chauffeur took her to church every Sunday. The rest of the time the car stayed in the garage.'

He sat down. 'Well, we've got the pleasantries over. I'm sure you didn't come here to talk about my family. Shall we begin?'

'How well do you know Charles Renshaw's wife?'

'We're acquainted. I thought it proper to attend her late husband's funeral where, you may recall, I spoke with you and your wife.'

De Silva let that pass for the moment.

'You appeared to lose interest in pursuing your complaint about Renshaw's treatment of his worker Hari Gooptu very suddenly. Can you explain why?'

'As I said when we met at the church that day, I had decided to rely on your judgement. I accepted you might have been right, and my complaint might do more harm than good. Don't rock the boat, eh, Inspector? I believe that was your advice.'

'Are you sure it had nothing to do with Madeleine Renshaw?'

'Why ever should it?'

'Because, Mr Tagore, I believe that you and she are far more than acquaintances.'

Tagore's expression was unchanged. 'That's nonsense, Inspector.'

'Is it? You were seen with her at the lake on the Friday before the Hatton cricket match.'

'Pure chance,' said Tagore, barely missing a beat. 'I had

143

forgotten. She was watching her son swim. We spoke for a moment or two.'

Not how it had looked to him, thought de Silva. 'When my wife and I met you at St George's church the same afternoon, you mentioned you would be leaving Nuala the following morning, yet you are still here. Why is that?'

'The case I was due to appear in settled. As I no longer needed to return to Colombo for the hearing, I decided to wrap up my mother's affairs sooner rather than later.'

'Why did you check out of the Nuala Hotel?'

Tagore laughed. 'Really, Inspector, I fear you subscribe to the popular view that all lawyers are made of money. I decided to conserve funds and move here for a few days.'

'As you were unexpectedly here on the Saturday, did you go to the cricket ground?'

'I was too busy.'

'Were you here all that day?'

Tagore nodded.

'Are you absolutely certain? And throughout the night?'

'Yes.'

'Is there anyone who can vouch for that?'

'No, you'll have to take my word for it.'

'I beg to differ. I saw you myself in the woods adjoining the cricket ground. You met Madeleine Renshaw there. It was clear you didn't want anyone to see you together. Were you planning how you would get rid of her husband? He'd found out about the two of you, hadn't he? He and Madeleine had a violent argument over your relationship. You brought me the story about Gooptu's ill-treatment and that bloodstained shirt hoping I'd believe Gooptu or one of his co-workers were aggrieved enough to murder Renshaw when it was you who had an even more powerful reason for wanting him dead.'

Tagore rose quickly from his chair. 'I won't listen to any more of this nonsense.'

De Silva was at the door before him, barring the way. 'You're not going anywhere, Mr Tagore,' he said quietly. 'I'm arresting you for the murder of Charles Renshaw.'

CHAPTER 18

Jane was out again that evening, persuaded by Florence Clutterbuck to attend yet another of her events. This time it was a charitable one. Although he was careful not to show it, de Silva was relieved. It would have been a struggle to hide his uneasiness from her.

Despite his fears that Tagore would become violent, the fellow had gone quietly to the station. Was the dignity he showed evidence of innocence or concealment of guilt? De Silva wasn't sure. At the station more questioning had proved fruitless. In the end he had left him in one of the cells and instructed Prasanna to stay overnight to guard him.

Over his solitary dinner, de Silva analysed the facts with mounting apprehension. Tagore had a motive for wanting Renshaw dead and he had no alibi for the night of the murder, but was that enough to prove he was guilty? If he had made a mistake arresting Tagore, there would be hell to pay. The lawyer would want his revenge. Clutterbuck would criticise him for being too hasty, and Jane would be angry that he had unjustly implicated Madeleine in a plot to kill her husband.

He pushed his plate away with his favourite spicy dahl only half eaten. Tomorrow, he would interrogate Tagore again, but it was going to be hard to catch him out. The lawyer was used to examining others and not likely to trip himself up.

* * *

After two late nights Jane decided to breakfast in her room. De Silva took an early morning walk in the garden before eating alone and driving to the station.

'Anything to report?' he asked Prasanna when the sergeant emerged from the back room, rubbing the sleep from his eyes.

'No, sir. He's been quiet all night. Now that you're here, may I go out and get some food for breakfast?'

'You may.'

De Silva went down the corridor to the cells. Tagore lay on the narrow bunk bed with his eyes closed. He opened them when he heard de Silva's footsteps and sat up. 'I trust this charade is over, Inspector, and you've come to tell me I'm free to leave.'

'Not yet.'

'If not now, you'll be forced to do so soon. You know as well as I do that you haven't enough evidence to charge me. Your case is flimsy, based on your ridiculous assumption that because we have spoken a few times, Madeleine Renshaw and I are having an affair. If a breath of that slur on her name gets out, rest assured I'll see to it that—'

'I've warned you once not to threaten me, Mr Tagore,' de Silva said with a scowl. 'I'll leave you now. My sergeant will bring you some food in a while. Perhaps you'll feel more like talking later.'

Prasanna returned with a breakfast of dahl and vegetable curry he had bought at one of the food stalls in the market. For once the spicy aromas didn't make de Silva feel hungry.

'Take some to Tagore,' he said. 'Then when you've eaten get back to going around the Ayurvedic shops. Nadar had better stay here this morning in case I need to go out.'

He frowned. 'Is something wrong, Sergeant?'

'The bazaar's full of talk, sir. Some of the locals must

have seen you bring Tagore in yesterday. I don't know who recognised him, but people already seem to know his name. They were asking me what's going on. One woman wanted to know if he had something to do with the death of the British plantation owner. I didn't say anything, and she laughed and tapped her nose.'

De Silva groaned. It was his bad luck that Tagore was taller and better looking than most men. Nuala was a small town and he stood out from the crowd.

Prasanna had left to continue his search by the time Nadar knocked on the door of de Silva's office. 'The prisoner is asking if he may wash and shave, sir.'

'Let him wash, but no razor. When he's done, bring him to my office. I'll question him there. I doubt he'll try anything but stay close in case I need you.'

Shortly afterwards there were footsteps and Nadar showed Tagore in. The lawyer's air of cold hostility made the hairs on the back of de Silva's neck prickle. He was glad that Constable Nadar was within earshot.

Tagore sat down without being asked. Notwithstanding his crumpled clothes and unshaven chin, he managed to look supremely in control of the situation. 'Your constable tells me you have more questions for me, Inspector. Fire away.'

De Silva was about to frame his first question when they heard a commotion outside. A moment later the door burst open to reveal Nadar. His eyes were on stalks, and he was panting.

'There's a British lady here, sir. I told her you were busy, but she's insisting on seeing you.'

Madeleine Renshaw pushed past him into the room. Seeing Tagore, she cried out. He jumped up and she rushed into his arms.

To de Silva's annoyance, he felt a flush rise to his cheeks. He went to the window and stared out of it for a few moments. When he turned back Madeleine had calmed a little and was sitting in the chair that Tagore had vacated, clutching one of his hands to her tearstained cheek.

Tagore's whole appearance had softened. 'I fear the game is up, Inspector,' he said ruefully. 'One at least of your suspicions is confirmed. Madeleine and I are in love. But neither of us are murderers. You must look elsewhere for Charles Renshaw's killer.'

'Ravi?' Madeleine's blue eyes were wide.

'Yes, my darling?'

'Then it's true that Charles was murdered?'

'Inspector de Silva believes that's the case.'

'How horrible!' She rounded on de Silva her expression filled with anger. 'How could you think Ravi would do such a terrible thing?'

De Silva swallowed.

'The police have to consider every avenue,' said Tagore gently. 'I was alone at my mother's bungalow on the night Charles died. That means I have no alibi. It's only prima facie evidence against me but coupled with what the inspector believed he knew about us, it's not surprising he was suspicious.'

His calmness amazed de Silva.

'What the inspector hasn't explained is why he thinks Charles was murdered. Obviously, he doesn't believe the diagnosis of a heart attack that Doctor Hebden gave you. What do you have to tell us, Inspector?'

De Silva hesitated.

Madeleine let Tagore's hand go. 'You needn't be afraid that I'll faint or become hysterical, Inspector. Nothing could be worse than hearing Ravi was in danger.'

'I must ask Mr Tagore to leave us to talk in private, ma'am.'

Madeleine looked to Tagore for reassurance, and he nodded. 'It's alright. We have nothing to hide now.'

When Nadar had led Tagore away, de Silva leant forward in his chair and steepled his hands. 'Your husband didn't die of a heart attack, ma'am. He was poisoned.'

'Then why did Doctor Hebden say he'd had a heart attack?'

'The poison the killer used is hard to detect. Your husband had a history of heart disease. The assumption wasn't an unreasonable one.'

She looked down, hiding her expression. 'Yes, old Doctor MacCallum often warned him that he ought not to drink so much and look after himself better, but he wouldn't listen. I tried to help, but our marriage became an unhappy one so soon.' She raised her eyes to his. 'Would he have suffered much?'

'I don't think so.'

'I suppose I had better start at the beginning,' she said after a long pause. 'Ravi and I met in Colombo after my first husband died. He had been ill for several months and his death, though tragic, came as no surprise. Some friends took Hamish and me in and that's how I met Ravi.'

She sighed. 'I missed my husband but from the first, I felt a strong attraction to Ravi and he to me. If only I had been more courageous, we might have married eventually. I'm afraid I was too much influenced by other people's opinions.' She looked at de Silva. 'Many of the British community, including my friends, held inflexible views on mixed marriages. I had Hamish to think of too.'

De Silva thought of his own marriage. It would have been so much harder to take the step if he and Jane had been younger and had to resist pressure from family and friends.

Madeleine took a deep breath and steadied herself. 'Then Charles came along. He was approved of by everyone – he seemed a kind man then. I did my best to make him a good wife, but as time went by, he changed.'

'Did you and Tagore still meet after your marriage?'

'No, I tried to forget him.' Her voice dropped to an undertone. 'But I didn't succeed. When we met again here, it was as if we had never been apart.'

She gripped the arm of her chair. 'I tried to tell him it was no use and I swear nothing has happened between us that I should be ashamed of. Then Ravi found out about the man Charles flogged. He was furious.'

'But why did he make the complaint so openly? Wasn't it rash to draw Charles's attention to himself?'

'It wasn't just that man Ravi was concerned about. He was afraid for me. Charles could be vicious when he was drunk. He'd threatened me on several occasions. It was probably a mistake to tell Ravi that. He wanted me to leave Charles. He thought that if Charles was charged with assault, everything about him would come out. I would be able to get away safely.'

'So did your husband challenge you about Tagore?'

'Yes, we had a terrible quarrel the evening after you came to the plantation. He said I could get out if I liked but if I did, he'd blacken my name. He'd make sure Hamish was taken away from me too. I wasn't sure if he could do that, but I was so afraid it might be true. In the end he stormed off. As far as I know, he slept in his office. The next day he kept saying how sorry he was. We were due to stay at the Crown that night. He said we'd have the day together with Hamish, but then David Leung arrived.'

Her voice faltered and de Silva waited while she composed herself.

'I never liked Leung. Even in the Colombo days I thought he was a bad influence on Charles. Oh, he could be charming, but he was secretive. He always seemed to have money, but how he made it wasn't clear. When we came up here, I hoped we'd seen the last of him.'

There was a knock at the door. 'Yes?' called de Silva. He didn't want Madeleine interrupted.

Nadar put his head in. 'Mrs de Silva's on the telephone, sir. Asking if you're here.'

'Tell her I'll call her as soon as I can.'

The door closed. 'Please go on,' he said.

'Leung persuaded Charles to go up to the Empire Club with him to play billiards. They were there most of the day. While Charles was away, I had a note from Ravi asking me to meet him. I said I couldn't, but when I took Hamish swimming at the lake, Ravi followed us. He wasn't willing at first, but I persuaded him eventually that it was best to leave Charles alone. I also told him not to try and see me again.'

'But you met at the cricket match?'

She lowered her eyes. 'Yes.'

Her head jerked up and her eyes were filled with tears. 'Ravi hasn't killed anyone, Inspector de Silva, but I have.'

A jolt went through de Silva. Was this the confession he'd been waiting for? If it was, he wasn't sure whether to believe it. She might simply have some idea about protecting her lover.

Instead Madeleine gave him a wan smile. 'I killed poor old Jacko. He must have heard Charles and me arguing, and he was so quick to pick up words. After I chased him away that afternoon, there was no sign of him for the rest of the day. I kept trying to reassure Hamish that he'd be back, but he would barely speak to me. In fact I was glad Jacko had gone. I was worried he might say things that made people suspicious.'

As indeed he did, thought de Silva.

'Charles always kept a rifle in his dressing room cupboard. The plantation doesn't have any near neighbours and he thought we might have to defend ourselves one day. He insisted on showing me how to use it so that I'd have a way of protecting us when he was away in Colombo for the tea auctions.'

She wiped her eyes. 'I hardly slept on the night Jacko escaped. It was nearly dawn when I heard him in the trees near the verandah. The maids always leave a bowl of fruit in the bedroom, so I cut up a mango – that was his favourite – and threw it as far as I could onto the lawn. By the time he hopped over to eat it, I'd fetched the rifle. I was shaking so much that I was afraid I'd miss.'

Her voice faded to a whisper. 'But I didn't. I killed him with one shot. Afterwards I ran out and wrapped his body in one of my old shawls. I ordered one of the servants to bury him and made up the story about the wild animal.'

A long shudder went through her, and her hands clenched in her lap. 'Now that you know everything, Inspector, you will let Ravi go, won't you?'

An abyss of silence gaped between them. She rose from her chair, her face chalk white. For a moment, he thought she would lose control and strike him then she slammed her fist on the desk with surprising force. 'You *will* let him go. I'll make you.' She glared at him so intensely that she seemed to dominate the room. Then with a swish of skirts, she turned and rushed out, leaving de Silva rigid in his chair, his ears ringing from the slam of the door.

CHAPTER 19

'Dammit, de Silva, what the hell's going on?'

He held the receiver away from his ear as Archie Clutterbuck's irate voice boomed out. 'My wife tells me you've arrested that damned meddling lawyer Tagore for the murder of Charles Renshaw and I'm the last to know! It's… it's… unconscionable!'

'I can explain—'

'Oh, you can, eh? It had better be good. You've made me look a fool and my wife is on the warpath. She's heard some infernal gossip about Tagore and Madeleine Renshaw, and she wants to get to the bottom of it. Mrs Renshaw has become quite a pet of hers.'

The assistant government agent's breathing quietened as de Silva ran through the events of the last few days as succinctly as he could. When he had finished, he waited, listening to the cogs of Clutterbuck's brain whirr.

'Very well,' he growled at last. 'Keep Tagore where he is for the moment. You may continue your investigation, but if you're right and we've got a murder on our hands, I'll have to give serious consideration to involving the police in Colombo. We may need their resources.'

A sinking feeling came over de Silva. Much as he respected his old colleagues, he didn't want any interference. The honour of the Nuala police force was at stake.

'But I hear the line's still down this side of Hatton,'

Clutterbuck said in a milder tone. 'I'll have to wait until it's fixed to speak to Colombo.' He paused. 'Make good use of your time, de Silva.'

Abruptly, the line went dead. De Silva pulled out his handkerchief and mopped the sweat from his brow. It was a relief to have more time. The problem was how to follow Clutterbuck's advice and use it well.

The telephone rang again. His heart thudded as he answered it. It was Jane.

'Shanti? Whatever's going on? Florence Clutterbuck has just called to ask if I know where Madeleine is. They were at the Crown this morning – she'd promised to take some raffle prizes up early – and the place was full of the most scurrilous rumours about Ravindra Tagore. Someone said he'd killed Charles Renshaw and you'd arrested him. Apparently, Madeleine went white and ran out of the hotel before anyone had time to stop her. She jumped into a rickshaw, and no one's seen her since.'

He struggled for the right words and her voice rose. 'Shanti! You don't mean to tell me you *have* arrested him?'

Once more de Silva went through the facts.

'I can hardly believe it,' said Jane sadly. 'I hope you're wrong. Poor Madeleine, she's gone through so much.' He heard her sharp intake of breath. 'You don't think she had any part in it, do you? Oh, Shanti, that's impossible.'

'I'm afraid nothing's impossible, my love. I'm not sure of anything yet. I have to go. I'll telephone you later.'

But for a few moments, he didn't leave his desk. A terrifying vision of Florence Clutterbuck in full battle cry assailed him. Madeleine might have gone to enlist her help in freeing Tagore. His blood seemed to fizz in his ears, and he had to breathe deeply until the sensation faded. As it did, he pulled himself together. He needed time to think in peace. Maybe he should go back to the plantation. It would remove him from the theatre of war and there might even be a clue he had missed.

* * *

The Morris purred along the sunlit roads. The soothing influence that driving always had on him exerted its effect, and by the time he reached the Five Palms he felt calm. He would begin by making one more check through Renshaw's papers.

To his surprise, he wasn't alone at the plantation. The black Daimler was parked in the yard. As he crossed to the factory door, he noticed that the bent wheel spokes still hadn't been attended to. He would never have left that kind of thing undone with the Morris. It was a pity Leung didn't take more pride in his expensive car.

He climbed the stairs to the first floor. As he entered Renshaw's office, Leung looked up from some papers he had out on the desk. 'Ah, Inspector de Silva. I was just going through Charles's papers, trying to find something that might help Madeleine. I want to salvage as much money as possible for her. I'm afraid I've had no luck so far. But as I'm here, is there anything I can help you with?'

Inwardly, de Silva cursed. He had hoped to have the place to himself. He forced a civil smile. 'It's good of you to offer, but I wouldn't dream of taking up your time.'

An uncomfortable silence fell then Leung smiled. 'Well, if I can't be of use, I'll leave you in peace, Inspector. In any case, I have an appointment in town shortly.'

De Silva moved aside, and Leung started down the stairs. As he watched him go, de Silva wondered whether he was telling the truth. When the footsteps had died away, he turned his attention to the papers that lay on the desk. Some were unpaid invoices and others were letters from impatient creditors. Nothing to suggest Leung was lying.

After an hour of sifting through Renshaw's disorderly filing system for a second time, de Silva was no further forward and growing weary. His stomach told him it was midday and a glance at the clock confirmed it. Downstairs, he went to find the caretaker to tell the man that he was leaving.

The caretaker was scooping dahl into his mouth with a big piece of naan bread. The spicy aroma made de Silva's stomach rumble even more. He walked across the quiet yard and got into the Morris. He'd stop for lunch rather than wait to get home. There was a curry stall he'd passed on the way that looked perfectly clean. He looked at his watch. Even with a stop, he could be back in Nuala by half past one. It suddenly occurred to him that someone must have put the plantation clock back to the right time for now it tallied with his watch.

On reaching the stall he paid for a drink of coconut water, some roti with vegetables and a bowl of curry sauce. The stallholder ladled out the food then picked out one of the big orange coconuts from the pile by the stall. He sliced off its top with one stroke of a broad-bladed knife and handed it to de Silva with a paper straw.

De Silva took his purchases to a table in the shade of a coconut palm and started to eat. The food was hot and good. It was a pity he couldn't enjoy it as much as he might have done with less on his mind. When he had finished, he went back to the Morris. As he drove on to Nuala, he wondered apprehensively what he would find there. He had nothing new to tell Clutterbuck and once the fault on the Colombo line was traced, it wouldn't be long before he involved the police down there.

Unconsciously, he eased his foot off the accelerator. His head throbbed with the effort of thinking of something, anything, that might turn the tide. It was his experience that quite often the solution to a case turned on something that had at first seemed insignificant. Was there some small fact he had overlooked?

He ran over his suspects' stories. Tagore's had the obvious

incriminating element that he had no alibi for the night of Renshaw's murder. Leung's, on the other hand, appeared to be watertight. Only one thing bothered him. It was strange that a man as fastidious as Leung had left unnecessary blemishes on his very expensive car. When he'd had the puncture repaired, why hadn't he asked for them to be dealt with at the same time?

He frowned. The garage owner had confirmed there was an invoice, but it might be worth asking why only the puncture had been repaired. He put his foot down and headed for Nuala.

* * *

'All our invoice shows is a repair for a puncture,' the manager said when de Silva asked the question. 'If there was anything else to do, the owner must have told us to leave it.'

'Do you remember if there was?'

The man shook his head. 'We have many cars through here. The mechanic who did the job might.'

The heat in the workshop was searing. The cacophony of hammers on metal, engines revving, and blowtorches hissing made de Silva's ears hum. He noticed a strong smell of petrol and engine oil as the manager took him over to where a mechanic had his head under the bonnet of a light-blue Hillman. He tapped him on the shoulder and spoke a few words then the mechanic followed them outside.

'This is the man who repaired the Daimler.'

'Some of the metal spokes on the wheel that you repaired were bent,' said de Silva. 'Was there any reason why you didn't put that right?'

The man scratched his head. 'Nothing on the wheel was bent.'

'Are you sure?'

'Daimler a very fine car, I remember it. Except for the puncture, the wheel was in good condition.'

'Once you'd repaired the puncture, did you fit the wheel back on the car?'

The man shook his head. 'No, there was much to do that day and Mr Leung came back before I had time. He said he was tired and didn't want to wait for the wheel to be changed over. He would come back another day. I put the mended one back where it had been in the place for the spare wheel.'

'I see. Did you notice anything else? Anything unusual?'

The mechanic pondered for a few moments then shrugged. 'The wheel was very clean.'

De Silva thanked him and returned to the Morris. He felt a mounting surge of excitement as a hypothesis took shape in his mind. If the wheel the garage had mended had no bent spokes, then it wasn't the one that Leung claimed had been punctured. Why would he lie about needing to change it? It could only be to explain why it had taken him so long to get back to Nuala from the plantation. Then there was the clock. He put his hand on the horn to clear a path through the traffic. This time he was convinced he had the right man.

At the station, Sergeant Prasanna greeted him with a triumphant smile. 'Nadar and I've had some luck, sir. Half a dozen places have sold pitta tea recently. When we asked about Mr Renshaw and Mr Tagore, none of the proprietors remembered anyone like them coming into their shop, but one did remember serving a man who answers to Mr Leung's description.'

'Well done, both of you. Come along, Prasanna. We're going to the Crown Hotel.'

* * *

In the Crown's grand lobby, de Silva strode to the reception desk and asked for David Leung.

'I'm not sure where he is, Inspector,' said the receptionist.

'Then find out.'

The man looked nervous. 'Perhaps you'd like to see the manager?'

'Stay here and keep an eye out,' de Silva muttered to Prasanna. 'If you see Leung, don't let him get away.'

He was at the door of the manager's office when he heard running feet behind him. 'He's leaving, sir,' Prasanna gasped. 'I tried to stop him, but he refused to wait.'

Watched by astonished guests, they dashed back through the foyer and down the steps outside the front of the hotel.

'Where's he gone? Can you see him, Prasanna?'

'Over there, sir.' Prasanna pointed to where Leung was already at the wheel of the Daimler. They hurried over.

'I must ask you to come to the police station with us, Mr Leung,' said de Silva.

Leung frowned. 'What's this about? I'm in a hurry, Inspector. I have a meeting to attend.'

'I'm not offering you a choice, sir. I have evidence that you poisoned Charles Renshaw and you've been telling me a pack of lies.'

De Silva saw a flash of alarm in Leung's eyes, but it was soon hidden. 'I haven't time for this nonsense,' he snapped. He put his foot on the accelerator and they had to jump aside to avoid being knocked down.

'We'd better get after him,' said de Silva quickly. They dashed to the Morris and de Silva reversed the car out of its parking place and jammed his foot on the accelerator. 'Hold tight, Sergeant! This might be a bumpy ride.'

The Daimler was already well ahead of them. In Nuala's busy streets, de Silva needed all his concentration to keep up and avoid the pedestrians, rickshaws, and bullock carts that got in his way. Dogs, monkeys, and chickens scattered.

The Daimler's engine was more powerful than the Morris's. Once they cleared town, thought de Silva, Leung would probably be able to outrun him. If he was to have a chance of catching up, he must stay close now.

Prasanna yelped as de Silva wrenched the wheel across and veered into a side street to take a short cut. They were lucky; the alley was quiet. The Morris emerged several hundred yards later with a much narrower gap than before between it and the Daimler. Moisture streamed from de Silva's eyes and hot wind stung his cheeks as they cleared town and headed toward the lake. 'Come on, come on,' he muttered under his breath.

Prasanna gripped the side of the car. 'Sir, what if the…'

The Morris sped into a bend. As it swung out of it, Prasanna's voice rose to a shout. 'Look out, sir!'

De Silva slammed on the brakes and the car left the road and ricocheted over the grass. In the eternity before they came to a halt, every bone in de Silva's body seemed to grate against its neighbour. Then there was a moment of stillness, broken only by a ringing in his ears that gave him the sensation that there was a long distance between him and the world. He felt for his heart and found to his relief that it was still beating. He heard Prasanna shift in his seat.

'Are you alright, Sergeant?'

'Yes, sir.'

A faint mist rolled from the bonnet into the front seats, making both of them cough. De Silva looked over his shoulder and saw the small herd of shaggy brown ponies drowsing in the middle of the road, sublimely unconcerned by the trouble they had caused.

Two sets of skid marks had cut deep grooves across the grass. One set ended at the Morris, the other at a coconut stall by the lakeshore. The owner was jumping up and down, gesticulating and shouting imprecations at the black Daimler that had careered on and come to rest a few yards into the lake. The water lapped at its front wheels. Steam from its radiator drifted gently into the air. Children ran to snatch the coconuts bobbing in the water.

De Silva and Prasanna jumped out of the Morris and ran towards the driver's side of Leung's car. He was slumped over the wheel, but at their approach he jerked upright. 'This is an outrage,' he said furiously. 'I demand to see your superior.'

De Silva smiled. 'You can demand all you like, Mr Leung, but you're under arrest for the murder of Charles Renshaw.'

CHAPTER 20

De Silva settled down in the railway carriage and prepared to enjoy the journey up to Nanu Oya. His two days in Colombo had been very satisfactory. His old friend and colleague there had unearthed the names of the men behind Asian Ventures, the company that was Renshaw's principal creditor. One of them was called Chiam See Tong, who also used the name David Leung. The company was believed to have links to the Black Lotus gang. Leung had turned informer in the hope of clemency and was now in the custody of the Colombo police force.

At Nanu Oya, his servant Jayasena waited for him with the Morris. As they drove the last few miles home, the afterglow of the setting sun was in the sky. Flocks of birds flying to their roosts made dark shapes against the fading red. He stood still for a moment on the drive at Sunnybank enjoying the peace after the noise of the city, then went inside.

Jane was reading in the drawing room. She took off her spectacles and put the book in her lap. 'I'm so glad you're back, dear. I was beginning to worry. Was the train delayed?'

He bent down to kiss her cheek. 'Yes, just outside Hatton. The driver and the guards had to stop for a herd of goats that had strayed onto the line.'

'What a nuisance. Now, tell me how you got on.'

He poured himself a whisky and sank into his chair.

Jane already knew some of what had been going on and now he was in a position to supply the rest of the pieces of the jigsaw. 'David Leung has confessed to the murder,' he began.

'Excellent.'

'It turns out that he and Renshaw frequented many of the same gambling clubs in Colombo. Leung soon discovered that Renshaw was heavily in debt. He saw it as an opportunity to involve him in an extortion racket, one of the Black Lotus gang's operations. I expect that an Englishman on the board of the company that fronted it was a useful smokescreen.'

He took a sip of whisky and sighed. 'That's better. Now, where was I?'

'The extortion racket.'

'Ah yes. Renshaw seems to have had the sense to step away from that one before he was in too deep. Eventually, he inherited the plantation and left Colombo. He tried to make a success of it, but as we know the place had been neglected and was in a bad state. He borrowed money but soon his bank wasn't so willing to lend. There were reports in the papers about the arrest of members of the Black Lotus gang, but Leung's name wasn't mentioned. There were also suggestions of insider leaks. It must have occurred to Renshaw that the leaks might have come from Leung, and he banked on it that if he was right, there would be underworld figures still out there who might be very interested in knowing about Leung's activities.'

He drank some more whisky before continuing. 'Renshaw contacted Leung to find out how things stood. Leung denied he was involved. Maybe he didn't think Renshaw posed a threat, but Renshaw didn't give up. In the end, Leung agreed to help him borrow money in return for keeping quiet.'

'So Leung set up the loan from Asian Ventures.'

De Silva nodded. 'He had an interest in the company and a pretty shady outfit it is. The Colombo force believe it has links to the Black Lotus gang. For a while Renshaw kept quiet and Leung thought he'd got away with it. But it was never going to be as easy as that. It wasn't long before Renshaw wanted more money. He was struggling to pay the interest on the loans he'd already taken out. Leung said no chance – Asian Ventures would never agree – but Renshaw wasn't prepared to take no for an answer. He told Leung he'd have to lend him money personally *and* get him out of the Asian Ventures debt.'

'Gracious.'

'That was when Leung decided Renshaw needed silencing – permanently. On the evening after the cricket match, he left Renshaw at midnight as he claimed. What he didn't admit to was that he came back and broke into the factory soon afterwards. He prepared the tea, put a lethal dose of cyanide in it and moved the hands of the office clock forward to fool Renshaw it was early morning. Then he woke Renshaw, pretended he'd come back to see if he was alright and persuaded him to drink the tea. The poison worked quickly. All he had to do then was drag the body to the withering room and haul it into one of the tanks.'

'It was clever of you to work out that Leung hadn't really had a puncture and he'd lied about spending time changing his wheel on the way home.'

'Thank you, my love. Yes, he deliberately damaged his spare and took it to be mended at the garage to make the story about being delayed by a puncture convincing. He was lucky too that Hebden put the time of death when he did. That helped to make Leung's story more credible. Of course, I'd never have guessed he was lying about the puncture if it hadn't been for those bent spokes. Luckily, even he can make a mistake. I must have caught him off guard when I asked which tyre had punctured and he forgot them. If he'd remembered, he would have told me a different one and I'd have been none the wiser. But he did make another slip.'

'What was that?'

'He didn't put the time on the clock right before he left the plantation. That was done later.'

'Just an oversight?'

'I imagine so. He must have been pretty weary by then. Renshaw was a big man to lift into that tank.'

'I was always sure Ravi Tagore's name would be cleared,' Jane said happily. 'And I'm so glad that he and Madeleine have nothing standing in their way now.'

'I suppose that's true.'

'Do they know everything that happened?'

'Tagore was down in Colombo, and he asked to meet me. We made our peace and I filled him in. I've left it to him what he tells Madeleine.'

De Silva thought briefly of the bloodstained shirt. He'd never mentioned it to Jane in case it upset her, and he wouldn't now. Tagore had had the grace to apologise for his behaviour on his first meeting with de Silva when he learnt it was David Leung who had arranged for it to be sent to him anonymously to add drama to the information about Gooptu. A clever touch that Leung had rightly expected would strengthen the trail to the dismissed worker.

According to his confession, Leung was also aware of Renshaw's jealousy over Tagore and that had been another reason for planting the shirt. He had anticipated that de Silva might find out about Tagore and Madeleine eventually and might suspect it was one or both of them who had plotted Renshaw's murder. If de Silva also realised that the shirt was a fake, he might conclude that Tagore was using it to deflect attention from their crime.

As it turned out, shortly after Leung was arrested, Doctor Bruyn's laboratory gave their opinion that the blood wasn't even human. They'd passed the shirt to the government veterinary department who thought it might be from a rabbit. Although he had warmed to the young lawyer, de Silva experienced considerable satisfaction when telling Tagore that. It might teach him a lesson about being too hasty. Perhaps the charitable view was that love had clouded his judgement.

'Why do you think David Leung stayed in Nuala? Wouldn't it have been better to get as far away as possible?' asked Jane.

De Silva shook his head. 'He needed to make sure that Madeleine agreed to let him sell the plantation on her behalf, so he had to stay to keep up the pressure on her. The money Leung gave to Renshaw to keep him quiet was in fact stolen from Asian Ventures. The company had no idea it had gone, and Leung wanted to get it back into their bank as soon as possible with no questions asked.'

'What do you think will happen to Leung?'

De Silva shrugged. 'That will be up to the courts to decide. He's offering more information about the Black Lotus gang, so that may help him.'

Jane smiled. 'I'm very proud of you, dear. I hope you know that.'

'Thank you, my love.'

He squeezed her hand and chuckled. 'Although I fear your Miss Marple would probably have solved the crime in less time.'

'Surely not.'

CHAPTER 21

It was a glorious afternoon for Florence Clutterbuck's annual garden party. The sunshine sparkled on the trumpets and horns of the brass band she had hired for the occasion. In the Residence's cool, spacious dining room, white-gloved servants dispensed tea, fruit punch, savouries, and cakes.

Wherever the British went, de Silva mused, they had the knack of recreating a little corner of England. One day they would leave and give Ceylon back to her people but for the moment the tendency had a certain charm.

He and Jane strolled around the luxuriant garden, admiring the plants, and chatting to friends and acquaintances. It seemed everyone wanted to congratulate him.

All at once, the brass band struck up a rousing tune and an anticipatory hush fell. 'Look,' said Jane. 'The government agent and his wife have arrived. Florence was so thrilled they've come up from Kandy for the occasion.'

The official car bearing Mr William and Lady Caroline Petrie, as the daughter of the Earl of Axford a titled lady in her own right, glided to a halt. Archie in tow, Florence Clutterbuck hurried to greet the honoured guests and a polite murmur of clapping rippled over the lawn.

Florence began to shepherd the Petries around those favoured enough to have a few remarks bestowed on them. General conversation resumed and de Silva saw Madeleine and Tagore coming in their direction.

Madeleine and Jane hugged. 'Such wonderful news!' Jane beamed. 'Have you set the date yet?'

'Yes, three weeks from tomorrow. The formalities will be at the Town Hall and then a small gathering at Ravi's mother's bungalow. We do so want you both to be with us. Please say you'll come.'

Tagore shook de Silva's hand. 'I second that.'

'In fact,' Madeleine added, 'I insist on it. We're so grateful to you, aren't we, Ravi? Jane for all her kindness and you, Inspector, for bringing us together.'

De Silva laughed. 'In a roundabout way, I suppose I did.'

'Will you stay on in Nuala afterwards?' asked Jane.

'Ravi needs to be back in Colombo for his work, but I hope we'll be able to come back here often. We plan to keep Ravi's mother's bungalow on. I love it already.'

'Will you sell the plantation?'

'I'll have to with all the debts that need settling, but I don't care. I'll be glad when it's gone, and I can forget that horrible time.'

Happy barking made them all look round. Hamish's new puppy was trying to persuade Darcy to play with him, but the older dog wasn't showing any interest. Hamish scooped the puppy up and carried him over. 'Hello, Mrs de Silva, would you like to meet Freddy?'

'Very much, he's gorgeous.' The black Labrador puppy was quite an armful already, all dangling paws and melting-chocolate eyes. He nuzzled Jane's outstretched hand with his damp nose.

'They've got ice cream inside,' Hamish said hopefully. 'Can we go and have some, Mamma?'

'Of course.'

They made their farewells and Jane and de Silva watched them walk away together in the direction of the house.

'I'm so happy for them,' she said. 'I know they'll have to weather a few storms, but we've always managed, haven't we?'

He nodded. 'And there's a lot more steel behind that pretty face of Madeleine Renshaw's than you might suppose.'

They noticed the Clutterbucks coming in their direction with the Petries. 'Oh goodness,' Jane whispered. 'We must be on our best behaviour, Shanti.'

But the government agent and his lady had friendly smiles on their aristocratic faces. Florence made the introductions, and they all shook hands. 'Congratulations, Inspector,' said William Petrie. 'Gratifying to show the boys in Colombo that you can cut the mustard up here, eh?'

De Silva thanked him and after a few more moments of talk, the Petries moved on. Another expression he'd not heard before, thought de Silva, but he understood the general drift.

'What a lovely dress Lady Caroline's wearing,' Jane whispered. 'And those diamonds! They must be worth a fortune.'

'I'd buy you even bigger ones if I could.'

She tucked her arm into his. 'That's very sweet but I'm perfectly content without them.'

'Thank you, my love. You know, if Ravindra Tagore is half as happy as I am, he'll be a very lucky man.'

'And if Madeleine is half as happy as me, she'll be very lucky too.'

Many thanks for reading this book, I hope you enjoyed it. The next book in the series is out now and if you would like to see a sample, please read on.

https://harrietsteel.com

Facebook Harriet Steel Author

Twitter @harrietsteel1

OUT NOW

DARK CLOUDS OVER NUALA

Inspector de Silva's back with a new case to solve when the arrival in the hill town of Nuala of the heir to an English earldom leads to a mysterious death. Throw in a mega-rich Romanian count, his glamorous countess, and an enigmatic British army officer and the scene is set for another intriguing mystery.

First published 2017

Copyright © Harriet Steel

CHAPTER 1

New Year's Eve 1933
Western Australia.

As the minutes to midnight ticked away, ever greater numbers of revellers crowded into the noisy bar. The dark-haired man limped back to his table with a glass of beer in his hand. Halfway there someone knocked into him, and he stumbled, lurching into a miner and slopping some of the beer down the fellow's jacket. As the miner jerked around, he waited for a blow but to his relief all that came was a gust of hot whisky breath and a muttered curse.

The young man waiting for him at the table was still on his own. 'They aren't coming,' he said miserably. 'I'm going to tell her I've had enough. When I leave, it'll be on my own.' He raked a hand through his hair. His forehead glistened and his skin had a greenish hue.

It was impossible to put things right, thought the dark-haired man. What was there to say?

Morosely, the young man reached for the bottle of whisky on the table and poured a shot into his glass. He drained it in one gulp and reached for the bottle again, but the dark-haired man pushed it out of his reach.

'Enough. We're getting out of here.'

Glowering, the young man tried to get to his feet but staggered. The table rocked as he grabbed its edge. The whisky bottle and the glasses slid off, smashing on the stone floor. He stared bleakly at the jagged pieces glinting in the puddle of whisky and beer, then almost toppled into the lap of the heavily rouged and powdered woman sitting at the next table. He clutched at her dress to steady himself, dislodging its neckline.

'You'll have to pay if you want to look down there, sweetheart.' She laughed and shoved him off then rearranged her cleavage. Her scowling companion started from his seat. He wore an open-necked shirt that revealed a burly chest. The sinews in his thick neck bulged and he clenched his fists.

The dark-haired man pulled a couple of dollars out of his pocket and pushed them across the table. 'Sorry about my friend, he's had a few too many tonight and some bad news. Please, have a drink on us. Happy New Year.'

The woman's companion hesitated then shrugged and sat down again. 'Happy New Year, friend. No hard feelings. But I'd get yer mate out of here before someone rearranges that pretty face of his.'

'Thanks for the advice,' the dark-haired man said dryly.

Outside, the temperature had markedly dropped. The young man gagged and doubled over. His companion helped him to the side of the road and looked away as he vomited bile and alcohol. When it was over, he handed the young man a handkerchief. 'Here, use this.'

The streets grew quieter as they neared the hotel. In the lobby the woman behind the desk glared at them. 'I hope there's going to be no extra laundry. I charge double, New Year's Eve or not.'

After making a stumbling ascent of the stairs, they reached a narrow landing painted a drab shade of brown which presented a series of doors. They stopped at the last one. It was unlocked. Inside was a pokey room. A light bulb with a cheap paper shade – the graveyard of years of dead flies – cast a glaucous light over an ugly table and chair and a bed covered with a faded red counterpane. The young man crumpled onto it and turned his face to the wall.

The window was shut, so the dark-haired man went over and struggled with the sash. Eventually it yielded, and air crept into the stuffy room. Distant cheers and shouts drifted from the centre of town. A million shooting stars and fountains of red, blue, green, silver and gold light split the night sky. As the first round of fireworks faded, welcoming in 1934, a succession of others took its place, each volley crackling and fizzing before it died, until a pall of smoke lay over the rooftops.

His heart hollow, the dark-haired man went over to the bed and looked down at his companion. Despite the commotion he was asleep. Very gently, he reached out a hand and stroked his cheek then brushed back a lock of hair that had stuck to the pale clammy skin. After a few moments, he returned to the window to view the display. His hands rested heavily on the windowsill.

Then fear seized him. Was it his imagination, or had something deep in the earth moved?

CHAPTER 2

April 1935
Ceylon

It was the day of the Empire Cup, the most fashionable event in Nuala's racing calendar. While he waited for his wife to get ready, Inspector Shanti de Silva strolled around his garden. Overnight rain had revived the rich soil and freshened the trees and flowers. His beloved roses looked splendid and the grass under his feet was a springy emerald carpet.

He turned to see Jane walking across the lawn towards him. 'Do I look suitable?'

'Of course you do, you always look lovely. Is that a new dress?'

She shook her head. 'Shanti dear, I've worn it dozens of times.'

'Well, it's very nice.'

'But I have bought something new for the dinner at the Residence tomorrow. I hope you don't mind.'

'As long as we still have money to eat,' he said with a grin.

She pinched his sleeve. 'You know I don't spend extravagant sums on dresses, and this is very pretty − a sea-green silk with a bolero jacket. I think you'll like it. I plan to wear it with my pearls.'

'I'm only teasing, and I'm sure I'll love it.' He offered her his arm. 'Shall we be on our way? It would be a pity to miss the first race.'

The Morris waited for them on the drive. Their servant Jayasena had washed and polished its smart navy paintwork and chrome fittings, and they gleamed in the sunshine. De Silva started the engine and the car crunched over Sunnybank's gravelled drive and turned onto the road.

'I've been looking forward to this for weeks,' remarked Jane, putting up one hand to hold her hat in place as they speeded up. Sunshine filtered through the green tunnel of trees above them, dappling the road with light and shade. 'Florence Clutterbuck says William Petrie and Lady Caroline will be there today. They're up from Kandy for a while and have brought Lady Caroline's nephew and his wife with them.'

De Silva didn't comment. The arrival of this nephew Ralph Wynne-Talbot and his wife Helen seemed to have acted like a stone tossed into the quiet waters of the de Silvas' sleepy little town. The Wynne-Talbots were being treated as the most exciting visitors to come to Nuala in a long time. He hoped they were not going to disappoint everyone.

At any rate Florence Clutterbuck, the wife of the assistant government agent Archie Clutterbuck, and self-appointed leader of Nuala society, clearly intended to make the most of the visit. It wasn't every day that her husband's superior and his wife bestowed their company on Nuala, let alone brought prestigious relatives with them. Amongst other things, Florence was organising a grand dinner to which everyone who was anyone in Nuala had been invited. De Silva supposed he should be flattered that he and Jane were on the list, although he wasn't keen on having to dress up for the occasion.

Jane sniffed. 'Well, aren't you curious to see them?'

He chuckled. 'If you want me to be, then I am.'

His wife reached across the steering wheel and gave his knuckles a brisk rap. 'You're very provoking.'

De Silva smiled and changed gear as he decelerated to negotiate the bullock cart lumbering towards them. It surprised him that his down-to-earth wife was so excited about the whole business. He concluded it must be an English trait to take such an interest in the British aristocracy, in which the Wynne-Talbots were, apparently, about to play a notable part.

Jane had explained to him several days previously that they were in Ceylon en route from Australia to England. In England they would be visiting Ralph's grandfather William Wynne-Talbot, 13th Earl of Axford, who was not in the best of health. His death, when it unfortunately occurred, would make Ralph the fourteenth earl and master of a large tract of the English Midlands. He would also inherit Axford Court, generally considered to be one of the finest stately homes in England. In the days of Henry VIII it had replaced the draughty medieval castle built by Guillaume de Wynne, a Norman knight who had come over to England with William the Conqueror. Henry had rewarded Guillaume's Tudor descendant with the earldom for his services to the Crown. The first earl had the good sense to keep his king's favour by building a house that was large and magnificent enough to eclipse those of his peers, but not so grand that it overshadowed the royal palaces.

Yes, Ralph Wynne-Talbot's prospects were bright: a great landowner and a belted earl with the surety of a welcome in the highest echelons of society.

'But one thing puzzles me,' Jane remarked when she had imparted all this information. 'I don't understand why Ralph Wynne-Talbot has no title. Florence was speculating as to why that should be, and even though I don't like gossip, she does have a point.'

'Why would he have one? I thought you said it was his grandfather who was the Earl of Axford.'

'Yes, but where an ancient family like theirs is concerned, they usually have more than one title. The earldom will be the principal one but any lesser one, viscount for example, is usually given to the male heir as a courtesy.'

De Silva shrugged. 'Perhaps there is no lesser one.'

'It would be odd. Florence also thinks it's strange that Lady Caroline has never mentioned her nephew up until now. I wouldn't expect to have heard about him, but the Clutterbucks have known the Petries for many more years than we have.'

'There's probably some perfectly simple explanation,' said de Silva, rather bored with the topic. 'Nearly there. I hope there are some decent parking places left.'

The course was already bustling with chattering, laughing racegoers, but to de Silva's satisfaction they found a good parking place. Racing was a popular sport with all classes of Nuala's society and visitors in saris and sarongs mingled with those wearing floral frocks, western-style suits or even morning dress and top hats. As they passed one of the refreshment tents, de Silva's acute sense of smell picked up an appetising aroma of cashew and pea curry. He and Jane had eaten lunch at home, but he must remember where the tent was. He could always find room for his favourite curry.

They made their way to the paddock where the horses entered in the first race were already collected. They circled and tossed their heads as if they knew that the race was imminent and were keen to be off. Their jockeys, mostly gentleman amateurs looking smart in their shining boots, breeches, and colourful silks, chatted to owners and trainers.

'I always think it's most ingenious that they find so many different combinations of colours and patterns,' said Jane. She pointed to one of the jockeys. 'I like the look of the gold stars on the blue background.'

De Silva glanced at his card and then over at the rails where the bookies had set up their pitches. 'He's riding number twelve, Firefly. The odds are a hundred to eight.'

'Oh dear, not much chance of winning then.'

He shrugged. 'You can never tell, although I agree it seems unlikely.'

'Oh, but it's a pretty name. Maybe I'll put on a few rupees each way.'

'Well, I suppose a pretty name is as good a reason as any. We'd better get over to the bookies then. The race will start soon.'

Unfortunately, Firefly finished second to last but the de Silvas' choice in the next race fared better, coming fourth. They were nearing the paddock to see the horses entered in the third race, the Empire Cup itself, when Jane shaded her eyes and pointed to a group standing inside the ring.

'Oh, look over there! It's the Petries with Florence and Archie Clutterbuck. The young couple must be the Wynne-Talbots. My, but she's lovely, isn't she? What beautiful blonde hair she has and so slim. He looks very handsome too.'

De Silva studied the young couple without a great deal of interest, but he had to admit that his wife was right. Mrs Wynne-Talbot was a stunner. Tall and slender as a birch sapling, she had hair like spun gold, regular features that would not have been out of place on a Greek statue, and delphinium-blue eyes. Her husband was equally striking but in a more robust way with dark-brown wavy hair, a strong jaw, and an athletic build.

Archie Clutterbuck noticed them and beckoned.

'Ah,' whispered de Silva. 'Here's your chance to meet this famous couple.'

'Oh dear, I wish I'd worn something smarter and what-ever shall we say to them?'

'You look extremely smart. And as for what to say to

them, there's never a gap in the conversation with Florence around.'

Jane giggled. 'That's very true.'

'Splendid afternoon, eh?' Archie Clutterbuck boomed genially as the de Silvas joined the little group that had formed around a fine chestnut mare. 'Mrs de Silva! A pleasure to see you.' He turned to the Petries. 'Do you remember Inspector de Silva and his wife?'

'Of course,' said Lady Caroline with a smile. 'How could we forget your triumph in the Renshaw case, Inspector? I hope life has been a little more restful for you recently. May I present my nephew Ralph Wynne-Talbot and his wife, Helen?'

Helen of Troy, how apt, thought de Silva. He hoped she would stop at being a beauty and not go on to cause a catastrophe.

They shook hands and exchanged polite murmurings. Helen Wynne-Talbot gave them a fleeting smile. Although she was tall for a woman, her hand was small and delicate and felt as insubstantial as a feather in de Silva's. In contrast her husband's grip was firm and his smile all-encompassing. To de Silva's way of thinking, however, the charm was just a little too practised.

Jane stroked the chestnut's neck and the mare snorted and nuzzled her hand.

'Are you fond of horses, Mrs de Silva?' asked William Petrie.

'Yes, when I was a governess in England, one of the families I worked for were keen riders and had a large stable.'

'We hope this one's in with a chance today. Our trainer tells us she's been performing very well over the gallops.' He shrugged. 'But racing's a funny old game, so I don't suggest you put the family fortune on her.'

Jane smiled. 'Perhaps just a little flutter.'

'Do you have many horses running today, sir?' asked de Silva.

'Only two. Kashmir in the second to last race and this one, Carolina Moon.' He touched Lady Caroline's arm. 'A tribute to my dear wife and a favourite song of ours.'

'And a delightful one, I must say,' said Florence. De Silva smiled to himself. Florence probably thought she had been left out of the conversation for quite long enough.

A voice boomed over the loudspeaker calling the horses to the starting post. Carolina Moon tossed her head and showed the whites of her eyes. Her groom brought her under control and the jockey mounted. As he gathered the reins and made ready to go, they all wished him luck.

The de Silvas said their goodbyes and walked over to one of the bookies. After brief deliberation they put a few rupees on Carolina Moon to win then went to find a space at the rails near the finishing post.

It took several minutes for the stewards to marshal the seething mass of horses into some kind of order, then the starter fired his gun, and they were off. The track had softened a little with the rain, but the horses' hooves still thundered over the cropped turf as their jockeys crouched low in the saddles urging them on. Slowly, the field separated into two groups, the leaders ten, then twenty yards ahead of the rest.

'See how her jockey's holding Carolina Moon back in fourth place,' said de Silva. 'He'll let the front runners set the pace then come through to win in the last few furlongs.'

Jane squeezed his arm. 'You're very knowledgeable all of a sudden. I hope that's right.'

'Of course it is. Haven't we had a tip from the horse's mouth?'

'With reservations, dear.' Jane raised an eyebrow.

The noise from the crowd increased as the horses streamed like a multi-coloured river around the final bend and into the home straight. 'What did I tell you? She's moving up!' De Silva struck the rail with his race card.

'I hope the jockey hasn't left it too late.'

The horses bunched together so that it was hard to see who was ahead, then by inches Carolina Moon took the lead. In a few moments, she was clear and streaking towards the finishing line. A roar went up as she passed the post.

'What a magnificent performance!' De Silva beamed.

'The Petries will be pleased. I hope we see them to congratulate them. And how nice to have such an exciting result when Lady Caroline's nephew and his wife are with them.'

'We'd better go and collect our winnings.'

'Oh yes, we mustn't forget those.'

'And after that let's go to one of the refreshment tents and celebrate. I'm beginning to feel a little peckish.'

Jane laughed. 'Alright, I suppose it *is* a special occasion.'

As they left the bookies, they met Archie who had also been collecting his winnings. 'Don't tell my wife,' he said. 'Florence doesn't really approve of gambling. I left her with the Petries and told her I needed to speak to someone on official matters for a few minutes.'

They walked back together to where he had left Florence with the Petries and congratulated them on the win.

'Yes, all very gratifying,' said William Petrie when he had thanked them. 'I hope Kashmir continues our run of luck. Now, if you'll excuse us, we must go and congratulate our people.'

Florence lowered her voice conspiratorially as the Petries and the Wynne-Talbots walked away. 'What a charming couple the Petries are, and the nephew will be an ornament to the aristocracy. But the wife!' Florence rolled her eyes. 'She's a funny little thing. Nothing to say for herself at all. I can't imagine how she'll manage as chatelaine of a great house like Axford Court. When she becomes Countess of Axford, she'll be expected to take her place in London society *and* take the lead in the county when the family is in residence. It will be essential for her to stamp her authority on her staff.'

When he wanted some light relief from his usual reading matter of the English classics, de Silva enjoyed the stories of P.G. Wodehouse. A vision of Wodehouse's creation, the stately butler Jeeves, floated into his mind. Florence had a point. As Jane would say, one would need to get up very early in the morning to stay ahead of Jeeves.

Archie frowned. 'That's enough, my dear. Given time, I'm sure Mrs Wynne-Talbot will grow used to her duties and discharge them well.'

Florence harrumphed and shot him an icy look. 'I only meant that one can't underestimate what hard work it is fulfilling one's social duties. I can vouch for that myself. The last few days have been so busy with arrangements for tomorrow's dinner.'

'And I'm sure it will be a great success,' her husband added quickly. 'Now, would you ladies like a glass of something? I saw Pimm's on offer in one of the tents.'

'That would be lovely,' said Jane with a smile. Mentally, De Silva relinquished his hopes of that cashew and pea curry.

They headed for one of the tents and found a table. Archie ordered a jug of Pimm's and for a while they chatted over their drinks then he stood up.

'If the ladies will excuse me, I think I'll go outside for a smoke. Join me, de Silva?'

'Certainly.' He wondered whether there was anything particular Archie wanted to talk about or whether this was just one of the informal chats he liked to engineer to keep abreast of things in Nuala.

They left Jane to listen to Florence on the subject of the following night's plans and to commiserate over all the work involved and went outside to find a quiet corner. Archie produced a monogrammed gold cigarette case and offered one to de Silva.

'No thank you, sir.'

'Ah, forgot. You're not a smoker, are you? Good of you to keep me company then.'

'A pleasure, sir. I'm glad of some fresh air.'

'Anything to report?' asked Archie when he had exhaled the first puff.

'Nothing important, sir. There's been the usual petty pilfering in the bazaar and a few disputes between stallholders but in general things are quiet.'

'Good, good. Glad to hear it.' He looked around before recommencing in a lower tone. 'I must admit, I agree with my wife about our visitor Mrs Wynne-Talbot. But it's not a subject to air in public. You never know who might be listening and heaven forbid such talk got back to the Petries. It would be bound to cause offence. I hear Lady Caroline's a great fan of her nephew.'

'The lady certainly does seem very reserved but as you say, she'll probably grow into her role.'

'She's a looker, there's no doubt. One sees why Wynne-Talbot was attracted to her. Petrie's asked me to organise a hunting party up at Horton Plains. We've a few others coming along. A chap from Romania called Count Ranescu and his wife among them.'

De Silva attempted not to look blank. He had no idea where Romania was and made a mental note to ask Jane. She was bound to know, and she would probably know the names of its capital city, its mountains, and its major rivers too. Geography was a subject she had particularly enjoyed teaching her pupils in her days as a governess.

Archie lowered his voice. 'Romania fought on our side in the Great War and it's still one of our allies, but the Foreign Office chaps are worried that Germany's taking too much of an interest in the place. It has substantial oil reserves and an expanding arms industry. The powers that be are keen to keep an eye on developments and when they heard that

Ranescu was coming to Ceylon for a spot of hunting, Petrie was told to play host and cultivate him. Apparently, he's got his finger in a lot of pies.'

He tapped the ash from his cigarette onto the ground. 'Our other guest's a fellow called Aubrey. He approached me not long ago asking if there was a party he could tag along with. He's on leave from his regiment in Calcutta. Came here to see a bit of Ceylon before he goes back to England. Petrie had no objection, so I told him he could join us. He seems to have done a lot of hunting in India, so he should be a decent shot.'

He paused and looked at de Silva shrewdly. 'Not a hunting man, are you?'

'Not really.'

De Silva refrained from adding how distasteful he found the habit of slaughtering game in the name of sport. It was an unpleasant fact of life, and the British administration was unlikely to abandon its lucrative system of selling hunting licences in the foreseeable future.

'To tell you the truth,' replied Archie, 'I'm not as fond of it as I used to be. These days I'd be satisfied with shooting for the pot – duck, snipe, that kind of thing. But I expect our visitors will be after bigger trophies.'

He dropped his cigarette end on the grass and ground it out under his heel. 'Right, time to return to the ladies.'

De Silva excused himself to pay a call of nature and was on his way back when he noticed Ralph and Helen Wynne-Talbot walking in his direction. They were alone and deep in conversation. Some instinct made him slip into the shadow of a nearby tree to avoid meeting them. His curiosity was piqued.

The Wynne-Talbots stopped when they were close to where he stood. Although he was unable to make out what they were saying, he had the impression that their exchange wasn't amicable. Ralph Wynne-Talbot's head was very close to his wife's, and he seemed impatient, speaking rapidly, and emphasising his words with jabs of his finger. Helen Wynne-Talbot's delphinium-blue eyes were red-rimmed and her lovely face pale as if she had been crying. Suddenly, her husband grabbed her by the wrist. She turned her face from him and tried to pull away, but he held on for a few more moments before he let her go. De Silva felt sorry for her.

He waited until they had passed on, then returned to the others, mulling over what he'd seen. He wondered what the cause of the problem had been. Whatever it was, it seemed that despite their glamour the Wynne-Talbots were not a happy couple. He considered whether he ought to mention what he'd seen to Archie Clutterbuck then decided against it. The state of the Wynne-Talbots' marriage was no one else's business.